Murder at The Campground

A CUBAN COZY MYSTERY

A TAROT AND VINTAGE CARAVAN COZY MYSTERY

ILEANA MUÑOZ RENFROE

Murder at The Campground

Murder at The Campground: A Cuban Cozy Mystery, Book 1
(A Tarot and Vintage Caravan Mystery Series)

Ileana Muñoz Renfroe

Copyright

❖

Copyright © <2023> <Ileana Muñoz Renfroe>

All rights reserved.

ISBN eBook: **979-8-9867450-4-6**

ISBN-Paperback: **979-8-9867450-9-1**

Library of Congress Control Number: **2023901931**

❖

Preface

❖

Welcome to "Murder at the Campground," the debut installment of the Tarot and Vintage Caravan Mystery Series, a captivating spin-off from the beloved Rosa The Cuban Psychic Cozy Mysteries. In this exciting new series, we follow the adventures of Rosalia Gomez, affectionately known as Abuela Nana in the original books, as she takes on new challenges and embraces her role as Nana.

Nana is a force to be reckoned with—a feisty and intuitive amateur sleuth with a knack for unraveling mysteries. With her trusted companion, and Moro her Shiba Inu, by her side, she dives headfirst into the world of crime-solving, uncovering secrets and unmasking culprits along the way.

But Nana isn't alone in her adventures. Alongside her, you'll meet Waltzing Matilda, a character as colorful and spirited as her name suggests. Together, they make a dynamic duo, bringing a touch of humor and warmth to even the darkest of situations.

As you embark on this journey with Nana, Moro, and Matilda, you'll find yourself immersed in a world of suspense, intrigue, and heartwarming moments. From cozy campgrounds to bustling small towns, each story promises twists and turns that will keep you on the edge of your seat.

So, sit back, relax, and prepare to be swept away by the charm and excitement of the Tarot and Vintage Caravan Mystery Series. Happy reading!

I.M. Renfroe

https://www.imrenfroe.com

❖

———

❖

Prologue

Rosalia Gomez had spent the last year trying to get her life back in order. It turned out it was a tall order.

Just when she thought things were going wonderfully, she and her nieta Rosa, were poisoned. Yes, you heard it correctly. Poisoned!

It happened when Rosa was preparing Colten Island for the annual Fashion Show. Rosa, every year created a new line just for the fundraiser. Last year was no different, only that one of the models was found dead right before the big event.

Then to make matters worse, another body was found. Nana started thinking maybe living on Colten Island was not what she had hoped for, only to learn that things were about to get worse.

In the midst of trying to figure out who the killer or killers were, she and Rosa were poisoned by someone she thought had been a friend to her. Needless to say, Abuela Nana as her friends and family called her, decided a change was in order.

Colten Island had been her home and place of business for several years now. She had always felt safe there, that is until recently.

Normally, she'd spend her days either working at her

shop, La Misteriosa Cafe or conducting tarot card readings for her clients. But lately she knew that taking a break from everything and everyone was exactly what she needed.

So, on an impulse she purchases a vintage caravan that comes with an unexpected guest. As she heads for a one-year camping trip she ends up with a nagging ghost and two cases that need her attention.

❖

———

❖

Cast Of Characters

- Rosalia Gomez (Nana) - 72, Can speak to the dead, tarot card reader
- Waltzing Matilda - 34, Romani/original caravan owner
- Moro - Nana's familiar (Shiba Inu) can speak to Nana telepathically
- Rosa - Nana's nieta
- Raul - Rosa's spirit guide
- Francesca - Nana's daughter
- Tomas - Nana's son-in-law
- Bill Yardley - President of the Miami Coastal Caravan Club
- Miami Coastal Caravan Club - Members own caravans or RVs
- Juana Sanchez - Tarot card customer and club member
- Eddie Sanchez - Juana's husband
- Miriam Rodriguez - Club member
- Pedro Rodriguez - Miriam's husband
- Reginald Thomas - Harding's Campground Manager

- Mary Clark - Reginald's assistant
- Beth Blackguard - Club member
- Roger Thompson - Witness
- Mario Wragg - Campground guest
- Sasha Tripp - Missing camper
- Alberta Tripp - Sasha's mother
- Sally Jones - Club member
- Leonardo Jones - Sally's Husband
- Linda McLean - Club member
- Valdez - Owner of Crystal Falls Campground
- Olga - Assistant to Valdez
- Yolanda Suarez - Manager of La Misteriosa Café
- Sheriff Alfredo Fisher
- Henry Finch - Masseuse

Chapter 1

❖

It had been a little over a year since Rosalia Gomez, known to family and friends as Abuela Nana, or sometimes just Nana, had unknowingly stumbled upon a killer. After her brush with death, the only thing certain was the fact that she needed to get away from everything and everyone. The solution; a new adventure. What new adventure, she wasn't quite sure of yet, but she imagined something spectacular. Una Aventura!

As far as an adventure goes, most people would have jetted off to Paris or traveled the world. Not Nana. After such a traumatic experience, she decided against that idea. She bided her time until she was certain she'd found just the perfect escape. And so, it all came to fruition when one of her friends and a tarot card reading client, after a year of constant nagging, convinced her to join the Miami Coastal Caravan Club.

Juana Sanchez, had just finished her tarot card session with Nana. She was beyond excited with what she'd been told.

The first card Nana had pulled was the Eight of Wands. This card indicated an unexpected trip in the near future. The quick journey would be safe and make her happy.

The second card pulled was the Eight of Cups. This too reflected an adventure, a classic card for travel. And finally, the last card read was The Fool. Although many think that was a foolish card, in reality, it signified a lively adventurous journey.

As Nana read her interpretation of the cards to Juana, she was over the moon with excitement.

"Nana, I can't tell you how happy I am with today's reading. It's hard to believe major changes are coming my way. Me has hecho muy feliz," Juana said rather giddy.

"Well, changes are definitely coming your way, and something you thought would never happen is going to come true. You know that I enjoy reading you the tarot cards. Siempre tienes muchas buenas sorpresas. So, I'm glad I could make you happy," she said with a smile.

"Yes, always lots of wonderful surprises. I couldn't imagine my life without you Nana. It amazes me, that I have been coming here to Colten Island for over a year now to have my cards read by you, *the* tarot card queen, *the* master extraordinaire. And, most importantly, that all of your predictions continue to come true," she clapped her hands in excitement.

Chuckling, Nana nodded her head and responded.

"That's so sweet of you to say, gracias. I just tell it as I see it, but you are correct though, it seems like yesterday when I first met you at La Misteriosa Café. Siempre un placer mi amiga."

"I agree, always a pleasure. By the way, since today marks our one-year anniversary, I have a proposition for you," Juana said with a twinkle in her eye.

Moro, Nana's Shiba Inu raised his ears and looked up in

anticipation of what Juana was going to say. Moro, had the distinct ability to communicate telepathically with Nana.

¿Nana, lo mismo de siempre? Por Dios.

Moro, por favor. We don't know if it's the same thing she's always suggesting. We'll just have to wait and see what she has to say. Nana smiled trying not to let Juana know she was actually communicating with Moro.

As a matter of fact, the only other people that could hear his thoughts were Rosa and her spirit guide, Raul. Nana's daughter Francesca had the gift, but had closed herself to it when Rosa was young and has refused to use it. Tomas, her son-in-law, couldn't see ghosts or hear Moro's thoughts, but he was just fine with that. He'd repeatedly stated that he didn't need to have any of those gifts. Especially, when he had his three favorite girls in the world with their own powers.

Nana had never told Juana or anyone else outside her immediate circle, that she could hear people's thoughts. So, Moro's suggestion was no surprise. Juana's proposition was indeed about her meeting the Caravan Club. Inevitably it was going to happen, she brought the subject of her group up often enough.

"So, Eddie and I were thinking how much fun it would be if you went with us this upcoming weekend to Marathon. You've always turned down long trips, but this trip is only a few hours away from here and it's only for a couple of days. We'd head back on Monday early in the morning. What do you think?" Juana was grinning from ear to ear and smiling, waiting in anticipation for a response hoping this time she would concede.

Told you!

Si Moro, tienes toda la razón. It seems you were correct.

This time Nana laughed.

"You don't give up do you?" Nana asked with a smile.

"Never! Sooner or later, I'll wear you down," Juana chuckled.

Juana had been talking about her club for months. A little over a year ago, Eddie her husband, had come home one afternoon all excited about a group of people he had met. It seems he had been having lunch in downtown Miami when he overhead a group talking about traveling the US in their caravans.

Eddie had always wanted to travel that way, but work and life had not allowed him the luxury. Now that he was retired, he thought it would be the perfect opportunity. He approached the table, apologized for listening in on their conversation, and asked if he could pick their brain about their upcoming caravan trip.

They welcomed Eddie's interruption, and explained they were indeed planning a trip. One of the men, told him about a club they all belonged to, and how much fun their previous trips had been. Eddie was hooked. By the time everyone was ready to leave, Eddie had officially become a member of the Miami Coastal Caravan Club.

He promised them he would talk to his wife and bring her to the next meeting. At first, when he told Juana about his encounter and the fact that he had joined the club, she thought he was crazy.

"¿Estás loco, un caravan? Pero Eddie what has gotten into you?" she asked twirling her finger around her ear to indicate he was crazy.

Laughing he kissed her, and then explained how he had always wanted to travel around the U.S. in a caravan, and now that they were retired why not try it?

What Juana did not know at the time, was that in order to travel with the group, they'd have to purchase their own caravan. But that actually turned out to be the easiest part, because the moment she saw the caravans in person, and met the club members, she felt a connection. She too was hooked.

Not surprisingly, in one of Nana's tarot card readings, she was told she would be meeting new people that enjoyed traveling in something vintage. The message had appeared rather cryptic at first, and Juana couldn't grasp the idea of traveling in something vintage. She had even dismissed the reading as Nana had maybe had an off day.

Little did she know that Nana was never wrong. Soon Juana and Eddie bought their first caravan, and never looked back. Since that day, they've spent most of their time traveling. And now, Eddie had recently been hinting about upgrading. Either changing it up and getting an RV, or if not, then another newer model caravan. So, today's reading was on point as far as she could tell.

Ever since their first trip, Juana had been trying to convince Nana to meet the other caravan folks, and possibly even purchase her own caravan.

The group consisted of mostly retired Cubans living in Miami. Although, there were a few transplants from New York and Vermont. One in particular, Juana thought would be a great match for Nana.

"As I said, my proposition is this… you join me and Eddie on our upcoming trip. We are taking the caravan, and a few members of the club are joining us on this trip. What do you think?"

Nana again laughed at Juana's relentless persistence. Mostly, because she couldn't imagine at her age having to sleep in a caravan. But just as she was about to turn down the offer for the hundredth time, Moro barked. In fact, he barked several times. To Juana, it appeared he wanted to go outside to relieve himself. To Nana, it was a different story. He actually was encouraging her to go on the trip. In no uncertain terms, he let her know she was working too hard at the Café and needed a break.

Taking a deep breath Nana looked at Juana as she slowly closed her eyes and nodded.

"Alright, tell me more about this trip of yours. Maybe I do need a break from La Misteriosa Café. It's been a while since I've had any vacation time, and maybe a mini vacation is exactly what I need right now," Nana encouraged Juana to tell her more about her idea.

Juana was so excited to finally get Nana to at least listen to her pitch, she just clapped and cheered out loud.

Laughing Nana tenderly touched her arm.

"Que cómica tu eres. Go on, tell me …," Nana encouraged her to continue.

Smiling, Juana explained they were first meeting the following Friday for Happy Hour to discuss the trip. There they would lay out their plan for when they were leaving, and the fall the logistics to make the trip a success. Juana made sure Nana knew she could stay with them in the caravan. They had it fitted with a bunk bed, since on occasion one of their grandchildren joined them.

It was a great way for her to get a feel for how they traveled. Juana hoped that would convince Nana to join the club, and possibly even purchase her own mode of transportation.

"You're going to pop a blood vessel if you don't calm down mujer, respira," Nana laughed.

"I know, breath. I just can't help myself. Tú sabes cómo you soy. You know how I am, and you know that I've been trying to convince you to join us for the longest time. It's so exciting, I can't help but be giddy," Juana smiled clapping her hands again.

"Yo se, incorrigible. Anyway, I promise to seriously think about it, and let you know my decision in a few days," Nana chuckled.

They spoke a bit longer, and then Nana walked Juana to the door.

Closing the door behind her, Nana took a deep breath. She liked having her clients come to her cottage on the island.

This kept the tarot card readings separate from La Misteriosa Café.

As Nana walked towards her kitchen, she thought about the possibilities. *It would be fun, and what's the worst that can happen? It's for just a few days,* she thought to herself. Looking over at Moro she smiled and nodded. Moro just barked.

"Guess you have nothing to say?"

I'm happy you have finally come to your senses. As I said already, a trip is what you need right now. Hey, I see you grabbing the leash. Does that mean we're going on a ride?

He ran around in circles excited to be going outside.

"Yes. I need to go downtown to pick up some items I need for La Misteriosa Café. Do you want to join me?" she asked as he'd jump at the offer.

Sure, why not. You know me, I looove to go out on car rides.

"Don't sound so enthusiastic," she said as she headed to the door chuckling.

You're just too funny. Do you not know me already? I'm always up for going outside or a ride in your car. So, let's go woman. Times a- wasting.

And with that he walked up to the door and sat waiting for Nana to open the door. Smiling she grabbed her purse, locked the door behind them, and headed to the car.

While on Colten Island, Moro didn't need a leash, but on the mainland, Nana made sure to have him on a leash. Once Moro got into the car, Nana started the engine and drove off.

Within minutes they were on the ferry. They were lucky this time as most often they'd have to wait in line. Once the ferry took off, they reached the mainland in no time.

Nana had been meaning to buy some items to decorate the Café. She even purchased some trinkets for those times that young children needed to be entertained. That always kept them busy while their parents enjoyed their meal.

As she arrived in the parking lot of the shop, she found a spot close to the entrance. She turned off the engine and reminded Moro that she'd leave the window open for him. But if he needed her, all he had to do was send her a message. She promised she wouldn't be long.

No worries, I'll be fine.

"Alright, see you in a few minutes, then we can walk over to the park," Nana said as she locked the door.

Can't wait.

Inside the store, Nana greeted the staff.

"Nana, welcome. What brings you to our neck of the woods?" one of the workers asked.

"Hola. Just stopped by to pick up some items for the Café," she said with a smile.

"Well, let me know if you need any help."

"Will do, gracias," she said as she walked towards the back of the store.

Nana looked around and after picking up a few small Cuban flags and chocolate cigars, she was walking back to the front of the store when she heard in her mind someone thinking about robbing the store.

Besides being a whiz at tarot card reading, Nana had other special powers. She had the ability to see ghosts, speak telepathically with Moro, and read minds. Something that often came in very handy.

Today was one of those days! Her ability to read minds was going to come in handy. As she moved closer to the man standing in front of the souvenir books, she could hear his thoughts.

I can do this; all I have to do is walk up to the counter and demand they give me all the money from the register.

Nana had only a few seconds to deflect the situation. The first thing she did was to send a message to Moro to come to the store telling him what was happening, and that she needed him to make sure he was near if things got out of control.

She then turned around, took out her phone, and dialed

911. When the operator asked her where was emergency, Nana gave her the address of the store. Then she did something unusual. She spoke as if she was speaking with a friend because she didn't want the man standing near her to know she was talking to 911.

"Yes, thanks Larry for doing this for me. I'll be here waiting at ...," she gave the address of the store again, and then briefly looked at the man and smiled. He stared at her for a moment and then lost interest.

As he walked away, Nana spoke softly to the operator so that the man wouldn't hear her. She let the operator know the situation, and that she needed her to send help. Instead of saying she could read his mind, she said she saw a gun. The operator immediately realized the urgency and dispatched the police.

Just as Nana was repeating the address of her location for the third time to the operator, the man started to retrieve his gun from his pocket. She dropped the phone at the same time Moro attacked. The man dropped the gun to the floor and cursed. Nana quickly pushed the gun away with her foot and nodded to Moro a thank you.

The manager came running to see what the commotion was about when he noticed Moro had the man pinned on the floor and close to him was a gun.

"He was attempting to rob you; Moro here seems to have the situation under control. I've called the police and they should be here any minute. With so many police officers patrolling the area, they should arrive in record time."

Just then police burst through the door. After they assessed the situation and spoke with Nana and the manager, Moro knew it was time to let go of the suspect. The man was immediately hand-cuffed, read his rights, and was escorted out the door. He kept babbling about the fact that the dog attacked him. Everyone ignored him and patted Moro thanking him for deflecting the situation.

"How did your dog know to attack this particular man?"

"He must have sensed the danger. You know that dogs can tell when someone has cancer. Maybe it's the same thing with a gun," she said as she shrugged her shoulders. It's not as if she could tell everyone that she called him over and once inside the store he knew what needed to be done.

"Well, maybe. Either way, I'm grateful nothing terrible happened, and that everyone is safe. Let me know whatever you need from the store, it's on the house," he said with a smile.

"Gracias de todas maneras, but there's no need to give me anything for free," Nana replied as she walked up to the counter.

"Bueno, está bien. If you insist."

"Always happy to help."

After Nana had paid for her purchases, she walked out to the car with Moro.

That was a close one.

"Yes Moro, I agree. It was way too close for comfort. I'm thinking this incident is a sign that I should definitely plan on going on the trip, maybe even take that year off, like I've been thinking of doing," she said mostly to herself.

Good. That's a great idea. Let's go buy a caravan.

Nana chuckled as she opened the door to the car. Not a bad idea, she thought to herself as she started the engine and drove to the ferry, not a bad idea indeed.

———

Back on the island, Nana went straight to her cottage, made herself a stiff whiskey, and sat down in her favorite chair. She realized she needed to gather her thoughts. After a few minutes, she opened her eyes and telephoned Juana to let her know she'd decided to attend the Happy Hour on Friday.

Juana was so excited to hear the news, she dropped the phone. Nana laughed. Once Juana had calmed down and given Nana all of the information of where to meet and what time, they said goodbye and before she hung up the phone, she thanked Juana for the invitation. She then made another phone call.

"¿Hija, como estas?"

"Bien Mami, gracias," Francesca replied

"I'm calling to let you know that I'm thinking of going away next weekend with Juana and her husband to Marathon."

"That's wonderful. I've been telling you since that nasty ordeal when you were poisoned and almost died that you needed to get away. Do you need me to watch Moro for you?"

"Si, gracias. If I decide to go either you can come and stay here, or pick him up. Let me know what works for you both."

"Wait, I just realized you said caravan. Are you actually going to stay in a caravan?" Francesca was surprised her mother would be so adventurous.

"Si, can you believe it?" she chuckled.

"No!"

"Something different," she replied.

"Well then, I'm very happy for you. And, don't worry about Moro. Tomas and I will take good care of him."

"Perfecto, gracias," Nana replied.

They discussed the trip a bit more and then agreed that Francesca would pick up Moro the following week and keep him for the duration of the trip. Francesca seemed to be in good spirits, so Nana thought best to keep the incident at the store to herself. *No need to worry her,* she thought to herself. The danger had been averted, and that's all that mattered.

For the next few days, Nana busied herself with the Café. By the time Friday rolled around, she was exhausted. For a split second she contemplated not going, but she knew it would break Juana's heart if she backed out now.

So, before she left the Café she decided to speak with Yolanda Sanchez. She'd hired her as manager a little over a year ago, and she'd turned out to be a wonderful addition to the staff. Always punctual and ready to get her hands dirty, Nana felt confident she'd be able to leave the Café in capable hands.

"Yolanda, can you come into my office for a moment please."

"Claro, Nana."

Nana closed the door behind her. She wanted to make sure they could speak freely without anyone hearing their conversation.

"As you know, we've discussed in the past my intention of taking a year off from running the Café. Well, I decided that before I would feel comfortable going away for such a long period of time, I'd try a weekend. I'm thinking of next weekend actually. Would that work for you?" Nana said waiting to see her reaction.

"Nana, you know you can count on me. I told you when we last spoke about this that I'd be available for as long as you needed," Yolanda said with a smile.

"Me alegro. Glad to hear you're still on board with running the Café during my absence," Nana also replied with a smile.

"Claro que si Nana. I love working at the Café."

"Good! Now that we have that settled, I was thinking to make it easier on you. I suggest you stay at the cottage next weekend. I have a spare bedroom and it would make it much easier for you if you didn't have to travel back and forth on the ferry. If you agree, I'll get you a guest pass so that you can also use the amenities on the island while you're here," Nana told her hoping that would make her happy.

Her rosy cheeks giving away her embarrassment, Yolanda only smiled and nodded: Words escaped her. Finally, she took a deep breath.

"Nana, I'm speechless. You have been so kind to me, I cannot believe you're offering me your home. I promise to take good care of it and of course, the Café. Como si fuera mio."

"I knew that would please you, and I have all the confidence that you'll do a great job. Oh, and don't worry about Moro. My daughter will be picking him up and taking him over to her house," Nana said as she stood.

Nana knew from delving into her thoughts she had nothing to worry about. Yolanda would indeed take care of the cottage and Café as if it was her own.

When they concluded their meeting, they both walked out together. Nana said goodbye to her staff and headed to her golf cart. She decided to take the long way home as the views were spectacular this time of year. The breeze coming from the Atlantic Ocean was wonderful as it hit her face. Breathing deeply, she thought about everything that had happened. If things went as she'd hoped, after the weekend trip she'd seriously look into purchasing her own caravan.

When she arrived home, she quickly changed into a summer dress and applied a little makeup. Satisfied with the way she looked she walked of out the cottage promising Moro she'd tell him all about the meeting upon her return. She climbed into her black SUV and drove the short distance to the ferry. As she waited to board, she thought again how her life had changed. The previous year she'd almost died, and now she was thinking of going camping. Odd how life can sometimes throw you a curve that ends up changing your life in ways you never imagined.

The guard signaled her to move her car into lane 2. When she pulled in behind another car, she turned off the engine. There she sat for the next few minutes until they arrived on the mainland. Exiting the ferry, she headed downtown to the restaurant, her excitement building.

As Nana pulled up to Eagles by The Bay, she was shocked

to see so many beautiful caravans and RVs. The entire parking lot was packed with different shapes and sizes. The more she saw, the more she was convinced she was in trouble. *Oh yeah, I can see myself in a vintage caravan.* Laughing to herself she exited the car and started to walk towards the main entrance when she spotted Juana and her husband.

"Hola Juana, Eddie. ¿Como están ustedes?" she called out as she approached them.

"Nosotros bien, gracias. Excited about our upcoming trip next weekend," Eddie responded.

Smiling, Nana hugged Juana and Eddie. They told her they'd been waiting for her arrival.

"We just wanted to make sure to be here to welcome you," Juana said with a smile.

"Thank you for the welcome party, but you know me, if I make a promise to be somewhere I don't cancel unless there's an emergency. Besides, I am looking forward to looking inside these caravans and meeting your partners in crime," she chuckled.

"I know, it's just … anyway, I'm glad you're here. Can't wait for you to meet everyone," Juana said as she ushered Nana towards the front door. She had been worried Nana would cancel and being there to welcome her was her way of making sure she didn't turn around and leave after she saw all of the caravans and RVs. They could be a little over-whelming.

Juana slipped her arm around Nana's and together walked up to the front door of Eagles by The Bay. Eddie stayed behind talking to one of the members who had just arrived. As Juana reached the door, the president of the club was looking out the window. When he noticed them approach, he smiled and waved.

"That's Bill Yardley. He's the current president of the club," Juana whispered to her.

Once inside Juana ushered Nana towards where Bill was standing.

"Bill, I want you to meet a dear friend Rosalia Gomez. Everyone knows her as Nana. I've convinced her to check out the caravans, and possibly join Eddie and myself on our weekend trip," she smiled as she looked at them both.

"Well, it's a pleasure to meet you and see such a beautiful woman interested in possibly joining our club," he said with a huge grin as he extended his hand.

"The pleasure is mine. I'm looking forward to meeting everyone and checking out the various caravans and RVs in the lot. In fact, I'm more excited than I realized," Nana replied with a huge grin as she shook his hand.

"Well, then as president of the Miami Coastal Caravan Club, I insist you sit up front with me. That way if you have any questions, I can answer them for you."

After a few pleasantries, Bill took it upon himself to introduce her to the rest of the club members. When the meeting was about to start, Bill ushered Nana to one of the empty seats. This pleased Juana as she thought Nana and Bill would be a cute couple. She hoped there would be a spark between them and it seemed that at least Bill was quite taken by Nana.

Bill called the meeting to order. They discussed the last trip, the October Foliage trip, and new business. By the time the meeting was over, Nana had made her decision. She let Juana and Eddie know that she'd be joining them on their trip to Marathon. Juana was giddy the rest of the evening and promised Nana she'd have a great time.

That night after Nana arrived home, she called Francesca to tell her all about the happy hour.

"¿Francesca, como estás?" Nana asked when she answered the phone.

"I was just thinking of calling you. I hadn't heard from you and I wanted to know how your Happy Hour went and if you had a good time? Are you finally convinced? Is glamping for you?"

"Well, as a matter of fact I am. Yes. I've decided to go glamping," Nana chuckled.

"That's wonderful! It's now official," Francesca said obvious from the tone of her voice that she was happy for Nana.

Then Francesca asked if Nana had spoken to Rosa. Nana knew that Rosa had been trying to avoid her mother because she didn't want her to freak out when she found out she was involved in a murder case.

Nana didn't feel comfortable keeping the truth from her daughter, but at the same time it wasn't her place to give out any of the details. So, she kept the information at a minimum.

"Si, hablé con ella hoy. Todo bien en Paris. Everything is going well in Paris. She's been very busy with the internship and the case."

She tried to then quickly ask her about her son-in-law in hopes she wasn't really listening.

"Wait! What?" Francesca screamed into the phone.

"Why are you screaming?"

"Why am I screaming? Seriously? You just said *a case*. Does that mean my Rosa is involved in another case? Por Dios."

"Calm down. Everything is fine. Rosa has Raul, and Storm surprised her with a visit, so she has him helping too."

Nana tried to sound as if it was natural for Rosa to be involved in a case, which in reality it was, since it seemed she was always either finding a body or trying to help the recently deceased move on to the afterlife.

"It better not, be worse than you are saying!" she demanded.

"Por Dios mi hija. You're always freaking out unnecessarily. Leave the girl alone. She's fine and in Paris!" Nana said sternly.

"Fine," Francesca knew she couldn't really argue with her mother, so she let it go for now. But she was already thinking that the moment she hung up with her mother, she was going to tell Tomas what she'd learned tonight. At that point she'd make a decision what to do next.

Nana moved the conversation away from Rosa and to the fact that she was going camping or glamping as her daughter had suggested. Francesca seemed to calm down a bit and was even excited to hear about her plans to go away with her friends.

"I'm happy for you Mami," she said in a sincere voice.

"Gracias mi hija."

They spoke a bit longer, and after they ended the call, Nana sent Rosa a WhatsApp message letting her know that Francesca was aware of her involvement in a case. However, she made sure Rosa realized she didn't elaborate on the situation, and warned her it was time to come clean with her mother. Otherwise, she'd do exactly as Rosa feared, she'd get on the next plane to Paris.

The rest of the week was a blur. Juana called Nana on Wednesday and gave her additional information about the trip as she assured her, she needn't bring anything except a small suitcase. They'd take care of everything else.

By Friday morning, Francesca had come by to pick up Moro, Yolanda had moved into the cottage, and Nana was ready to head out the door. Once she double checked the cottage one last time and stopped by La Misteriosa Café, Nana drove to the ferry. They'd agreed that the best place to meet would be Juana's house. That way, Nana could leave her car there over the weekend.

When she arrived, Eddie was outside checking the caravan. Nana admired the exquisite workmanship. He smiled knowing quite well how she felt. Eddie offered to give her a tour as he talked incessantly about the caravan, the extra features they installed, and the history of how they acquired the caravan. The more he spoke the more enamored Nana became with the whole idea of owning a vintage caravan and traveling around the country on her much-anticipated adventure.

Juana and Eddie's caravan had been remodeled completely with a Cuban flair and updated amenities. The perfect home away from home.

Once they finished packing the car, they piled in and Eddie started the engine of the SUV. Nana looked back several times to make sure the caravan was still attached. Juana knew exactly what she was thinking.

"Don't worry. The first time Eddie and I took the caravan on a trip I kept looking back to make sure it hadn't become unhinged. It's fine there, trust me. That thing isn't going anywhere. So, tell me como te sientes?" Juana asked.

"I'm feeling great. I'm really happy I decided to join you both," Nana placed her hands on Eddie and Juana's shoulders.

"Well, sit back and relax. The fun begins the moment we arrive at the campground," Eddie replied and raised the music. Celia Cruz was singing one of her famous songs. They all joined in singing the lyrics. Before she realized, they had arrived at the campground.

Eddie stopped at the main entrance, showed them his license and credit card. Once he was checked-in, he was given a pass and a map of where to park the caravan. The gate opened up and he drove towards the right, alongside the water, until he reached his spot B434. He backed up the caravan and they all got out of the car. Eddie then unhitched the caravan from the truck and secured it with chocks.

During this time, Nana asked questions as he worked. *Seems simple enough*, she thought to herself.

"What's next?"

Eddie explained he needed to connect the electric hook

up. After the outside was all set up, then they needed to move to the inside of the caravan.

"We have to set up the kitchen. Here, see... I'll open the sink and the cooker, and make sure all of the taps are closed. Once that's done, I can fill the water tanks," Eddie said to Nana.

"I can definitely do this on my own."

"You don't have to do it alone unless you don't travel with us. We can help you set up your caravan until you feel comfortable doing it yourself. If not us, there's always someone from the club willing to help."

"Wonderful! I'm actually leaning towards purchasing my own vintage caravan," Nana said with a smile knowing Juana would flip. Sure enough.

"YEAH! I knew you'd be hooked the moment you experienced traveling in a caravan. I can't tell you how happy I am that you'll be buying your own caravan. Eddie has a couple of great contacts he can share with you that can help you find your own special caravan," Juana said as she did a salsa dance move indicating how happy she was at the moment.

Hardy's Campground was a great place to visit. It had a pool, daily activities, and a pier that stretched far out into the ocean. By late evening, all of the club members had set up their RVs and caravan, and then everyone headed to Bill's RV where the rest of the members congregated.

"So, Nana, what do you think so far about our wonderful club," Sally, one of the club members, said with obvious sarcasm.

Nana noticed the tone in her voice and wondered what that was all about. Instead, though, she replied that she was enjoying herself so much that she'd decided to purchase her own vintage caravan.

Sally just smirked, mumbled something, and walked away. Her husband Leonardo, told Nana to ignore his wife's remark. He mentioned the fact his wife hadn't wanted to come on this trip, and because he had insisted, she was determined to make his life miserable. He laughed, and the rest of the people sitting around laughed along with him.

Once she made sure Sally was out of earshot, Miriam, another of the members spoke.

"She's always like that. Every trip she starts off in a bad mood, and then by the end of the night she's perfectly fine."

Several people nodded. Looking over at Leonardo she asked why he insisted on bringing her if it was apparent to everyone, that she really would be happier staying at home.

"Oh, you have no idea. I ask her every time if she really wants to come on the trip, and every time I expect her to refuse, she turns around and says yes. Then once we get to our destination, she becomes moody telling everyone I insisted she come until it passes. I've given up trying to figure out that woman," Leonardo said as he shrugged his shoulders.

Just then, Pedro, Miriam's husband approached the group with a cooler filled with margarita cocktails.

"Party time!"

All thoughts of Sally were forgotten, and by the time she returned to the group, she was smiling and very chatty. By the time the evening had wound down, Nana had made new friends, danced the night away, and agreed to have lunch with Bill the following day.

A moody club member, a supply of delicious margaritas, and a date. Definitely a very interesting night, Nana thought to herself as she drifted off to sleep.

❖

———

❖

Chapter 2

❖

When Saturday morning rolled around, Nana felt refreshed. She had slept like a baby and was ready to tackle the new day. Quietly, as to not disturb Juana and Eddie, she changed and headed out to get a Cafécito from the food truck that was stationed at the main entrance to the campground.

"Buenos dias. What can I get for you on this glorious Saturday morning?"

"Indeed. It is a lovely morning. Let's see, I think I'll have a Cafécito, una croqueta, y huevos rancheros to go please."

"Great choices."

Nana paid for her order and was told to have a seat on one of the empty benches that her food would be ready shortly. As she looked around, she noticed a large motorhome pull up to the main entrance. Then she noticed Sally walk up to the side door and climb inside. A few minutes later she exited the motorhome and walked towards the food truck unaware that Nana had seen her.

Pretending she hadn't noticed her, Nana looked down until she could tell Sally was nearby.

"Good morning, Sally, how are you this beautiful morning?" Nana asked looking directly into her eyes.

"Fabulous. I couldn't be better. If you'll excuse me, I have to place my order," Sally said and walked away before Nana could respond.

After placing her order, Sally stood to the side texting on her phone. Nana wondered if it had anything to do with whomever was driving the motorhome. But she dismissed the thought of getting involved.

When her order was called, Nana decided to head back to the caravan and sit outside in one of the lounge chairs. Too much mental chatter was giving her a headache.

Most of the time, Nana blocked everyone's thoughts. But sometimes, it was so strong it was inevitable that bits and pieces would get through. She couldn't help but circle back to Sally. Something was definitely going on with her and whatever it was, Nana didn't want any part of it.

Just as she was about to sip her Cafécito she noticed a shadow had blocked the sun. Looking up, she realized Linda was standing looking at her. She'd met her briefly the previous night while they were enjoying margaritas. *Well, I guess I'm not going to be able to have my breakfast after all,* she thought to herself as she smiled.

"Good morning, Nana. I'm sorry to interrupt, but I just wanted to see how you were doing this morning?"

"I'm doing great, thank you for asking."

"Mind if I sit down?" Linda asked, and sat without waiting for a response.

"Of course, by all means," Nana said despite her having already taken a seat.

Nana was patient as she waited for her to say whatever it was, she was there to say. Linda sat without uttering a word;

instead, she sighed. Feeling awkward and wanting to eat her breakfast, Nana figured she might as well ask what she needed. Otherwise, she'd never be able to finish her meal.

"Is everything alright? Do you need something?"

"Yes, sorry. I was just thinking here I am *again,* alone."

"I understand my dear. I am sorry about Paul." Oops Nana realized the moment she said it that Linda had not spoken his name out loud.

"How do you know Paul?" Linda asked in a suspicious manner.

"You mentioned him last night."

"I did? I don't remember talking about him, but maybe I did. Well, yes, I'm unhappy right now. I didn't expect us to breakup. Everything was going well until he started to get serious. All I wanted was to have fun, you know." She didn't finish the sentence.

What she thought was something totally different.

That conniving son of a... how could he leave me for a younger woman. I hate him for making me feel used. She looked directly at Nana. *If the rumors are correct, then this woman can tell me through those tarot cards of hers how to win him back.*

Wow, such anger. Now, I see why she stopped by the caravan! Nana thought to herself as she flinched at the angry words. Maybe doing a reading was what she needed to let go of this Paul guy.

"Well, I'm not certain if this will help, but how would you like for me to do a tarot card reading for you? It might be just what you need right now, to give you a hint of the next person you're going to meet."

"You read tarot cards?" Linda feigned a surprised reaction by covering her mouth with her hands.

From the time Nana was a little girl, she had been playing with the cards. At first, she just looked at the pictures, but soon it was obvious she was born with a gift. Whenever she turned over a card and someone was close to her, she'd say what came to mind. Every time she said something the recipient gasped in acknowledgment that whatever was being told to them was correct. Ever since then, Nana had read the tarot cards for so many people she'd lost track of how many.

Now Linda sat up straight and paid attention. Laughing, Nana told her she'd dabbled in tarot card reading. She needed to make certain to make light of the situation so that Linda did not realize she had read her mind. So, what she didn't say was she was a whiz, and when a tarot card was not clear in its meaning, she tapped into what they were thinking to get the full picture.

"Please. Yes!"

"Alright, let me finish my breakfast and I'll do a reading in about an hour. I need a little bit of time to get into the zone."

"Perfect. I'll see you later this morning." Linda stood and waved as she walked away.

Nana was finally ready to enjoy her breakfast when she heard loud yelling. Startled, she stood and walked to the back of the caravan where she could see Miriam arguing with her husband. The argument had something to do with being betrayed. Somewhat frustrated she walked back to her lounge chair and took a deep breath hoping she could now sit down to enjoy her breakfast. Unfortunately, that thought was short lived.

Por Dios. Am I not going to be able to eat my food? Nana thought to herself as Eddie and Juana emerged from the caravan.

"What's going on?" Juana asked, looking around to find the source of the yelling. Nana shrugged.

First Sally, then Linda, then Miriam arguing with her husband? This was a circus. Now, to make matters worse there was another person arguing. Nana couldn't help but wonder if coming here this weekend had been such a good idea. If this was the behavior she was going to have to deal with on her trips, then joining the group or even purchasing a caravan was out of the question.

"Really now this is quite unacceptable. I didn't come here to be treated in this manner. I want you to tell me immediately who complained?" Beth Blackguard, one of the club members demanded.

As Reginald Thomas, Harding's Campground Manager, was about to answer, she screamed over at Juana.

"Juana, did you complain about me?" Beth yelled.

"Me? I just woke up Beth. What are you talking about?"

Ignoring her, she went back to screaming at Reginald.

"Please calm down, BB."

"You can no longer call me BB. Refer to me as Beth Blackguard."

Reginald was surprised by Beth's sudden change of heart. He perceived their relationship to be without question one of love, so now that she was acting irrationally, he was confused. They had been seeing each other off and on for the past two years. Although, they had their ups and downs, for the most part it was a fun and loving relationship.

Yes, it was a fact someone in the campground had complained about the noise coming from her RV. He understood how much she enjoyed listening to music as loud as possible, but he had told her numerous times she couldn't do that in a campground. There were rules, but she continued to ignore him. Now, here he was trying to defuse the situation and it was only getting worse. Maybe he needed to reconsider their relationship as it was causing more problems for him than it was worth.

As more and more campers stopped to watch the commotion, Reginald knew he had to do something fast. Whispering in Beth's ear, he told her he would speak with her later after everyone was gone. This seemed to do the trick.

"Fine. For now, I'll quiet down. But mark my words! If I don't get what I want, someone is going to pay!" she said as she stormed back into her caravan and slammed the door.

"Sorry for the disruption folks. Nothing more to see here. Thank you," Reginald said as he walked over to his golf cart and drove off in the direction of the office.

At that point Nana had given up on the idea of eating a warm breakfast. Her solution, go into the caravan and heat up her Cafécito and eggs. Juana followed.

"I'm so very sorry Nana. All of this bickering is not normal. At least not with our group. I don't know what's going on, maybe it's a full moon," she said embarrassed at the whole situation.

"Don't worry. It's not your fault some people are so passionate they can't control themselves," Nana chuckled.

"Well, thank you for being such a good sport," Juana replied with a smile.

"Of course. Tell me something though, what's the story with Linda? Oh, and Sally."

"I don't know too much about Linda. She's usually a happy camper as they say, but of late I have noticed she's not herself. Maybe you should do a tarot card reading for her?" Juana suggested.

"You read my mind. I actually offered a reading. She's coming by later this afternoon," Nana replied.

"Wait, don't you have a lunch date with Bill?" Juana asked wondering if Nana had canceled her plans.

"Don't worry. I haven't forgotten, I just figured I could do the reading before I headed out to lunch."

"Oh alright."

That was close. It would have been a shame if she'd canceled her lunch with Bill.

"Maybe I should cancel."

"No!" Juana was so vocal about it that Nana had no choice but to laugh.

"I see you feel very strongly about me going to lunch with Bill. May I ask why?"

"You see, Eddie and I feel that you and Bill would make a great couple. So, we're hoping you both hit it off and start dating," she replied with a twinkle in her eye.

Laughing Nana nodded and just threw her hands up in the air. *Por Dios.*

"Don't be mad."

"I'm not mad, you're just incorrigible. But don't worry, I still love you," Nana went over and hugged Juana.

Juana relaxed and sighed; glad Nana was not upset. *They really would make a great couple.*

"Alright, enough about Bill. I'm going to heat up my breakfast and sit here quietly until I'm done eating. Go be with your husband and we'll talk later."

Smiling she turned towards the door.

"See you later."

After Juana had left, Nana took a deep breath and thought about everything that had happened so far. Something was definitely in the air and she needed to concentrate and focus before it was too late. Maybe she could control the outcome … who was she kidding. Danger was close - she could feel it in her bones and there was nothing she could do about it.

Just as Nana finished her breakfast there was a knock on the door. Emptying her paper plate and napkin in the garbage, she went to open the door. There he stood Bill grinning from ear to ear.

"Morning to you Nana. How are you doing on this wonderful Saturday morning?"

The second person to use those same exact words. Strange.

"Buenos dias, Bill. Well, I can tell you that this has been an interesting morning so far. But I see you're in good spirits today. Would you like to come inside?"

"Yes, thank you."

Bill climbed into the caravan and closed the door behind him. As he went to sit in the empty chair, he asked her what she meant by an interesting morning. Nana was cautious and since she didn't want to come across as a hysterical woman, she only mentioned the argument between Beth and Reginald.

"Oh, those two. They've been like that for as long as I can remember. After a couple of hours, they act as if nothing happened. You don't have to worry, besides I'm here to protect you.

Oh, boy did he just say he's here to protect me? Red flags started going off in Nana's head. That was all she needed. Maybe going to lunch with Bill was not a good idea. She didn't see a spark and if there was no interest there, she shouldn't encourage something that was never going to go anywhere.

"You know Bill, I was thinking maybe this lunch of ours should be postponed for another day. I'm feeling rather tired and don't really want to leave the area," Nana said as she shrugged her shoulders.

"No!" He practically screamed the word.

"Sorry, I meant don't be silly. I can bring lunch here and we can eat outside," he replied smiling. A smile that appeared strained.

"Since this trip is your first-time camping, especially with our group, I wanted to make it special for you. So, if you are in agreement, I'll return around noon."

He was rather persistent.

"If you insist. I must tell you though that I have a 2:00 pm appointment I cannot miss. That shouldn't be a problem, correct?" now Nana sounded stern.

"Oh, I see. 2:00 pm, you say? It's just that I was hoping we'd actually spend the afternoon together."

That's never going to happen, she thought to herself.

"I'm sorry. You invited me to *lunch,* and that to me meant an hour or two at the most."

Nana stood her ground. When it was apparent, she was not going to change her mind, Bill agreed.

"You are correct. I was just jumping the gun. We'll have lunch at noon, and I promise to be out of here before your appointment," Bill said with a smile.

Nana stood and opened the door to the caravan. Bill leaned in to give her a kiss on the cheek and she recoiled. Smiling she turned him around and ushered him out the door. She wasn't quite sure why she lied about her appointment time as it was actually at 11:00 am, but something told her to make it impossible for him to stay the entire day.

After Bill had gone, Nana reminded herself she needed to concentrate on the task at hand. Reaching for her tarot cards, she shuffled them several times and then placed one card faced down.

Out loud she asked if danger was afoot. Reaching out to turn the card over she hesitated and closed her eyes. Nana realized she didn't need a card to tell her what she already knew. Regardless, she turned the card over. She was expecting the Five of Cups or even the Seven of Swords. But not the Magician. The magician was a master manipulator who created the reality he or she wanted. Interesting.

E ddie and Juana returned to the caravan as Nana was putting her tarot cards away. They were chatting about a new place in town that was all the rave. Juana was excited and wanted to know if Nana would accompany them to the grand opening.

The Point, a bar at the end of the island, had been newly renovated, and they were doing a soft opening for family and friends.

Nana gracefully declined telling them she needed to make some phone calls before her tarot card reading and her lunch date with Bill, and wouldn't have time if she went to the opening.

"No worries, te llamo después to see if once you're done, and not too tired, you want to join us. We plan on being there for a while"

"Está bien Juana. Have fun you guys. Hasta luego."

"Nos vemos, bye."

Once they were gone, Nana got to work. She pulled out her incense. Patchouli was the best one to use when you wanted to attract your spirit guides. Then she placed two incense sticks in their special holder, lit the incense and inhaled. The next thing she did was take out the special tarot cards she used for reading her clients. These were wrapped in black silk. Her personal tarot cards were wrapped in white silk.

She shuffled her cards, and then stacked them into one pile. For added protection she went and grabbed a clear glass and filled it with water placing it on the table next to the incense.

When she was ready, she concentrated on Linda. Nana had decided she needed to center herself knowing quite well that the session with her was going to be difficult. She debated whether or not to do a reading for Bill. In the end, she settled for going to lunch and at that point would see how that went before she tried to do a tarot card reading on him.

Ready or not here I come, she thought to herself as she shuffled the cards once more. Turning over the first card, Nana cocked her head. *Interesting, very interesting,* she thought as she continued to concentrate.

The first card she drew was the Ten of Swords. That was not a good start as this card usually meant you were powerless, a victim, and mostly certainly will hit rock bottom soon.

The next card she turned over was the Seven of Swords.

This card signified betrayal and cheating. Nana wondered if all of the ruckus in her head was because her lover had left her or if it meant something more sinister? If so, that would explain why she'd pulled this particular card.

The final card was the Two of Swords. Nana took a deep breath and said a silent prayer. In all the time she'd been doing tarot card readings, never had she'd encountered these three cards straight in a row. And, the fact that this card specifically talked about one's mental health was very worrisome.

Nana stopped what she was doing immediately and meditated. She needed to cleanse herself of any negativity. Something had to be done, but what? She needed to focus so that she could come up with the best course of action.

Before she could delve any further into the situation, her timer went off. It was time to get ready for Linda.

By the time Linda arrived, Nana was ready for the session. She understood the moment she opened the door that the Miami Coastal Caravan Club had more drama than a Cuban soap opera.

"I must admit I'm a bit nervous. I've never had my cards read and don't know what to expect," Linda said out loud, but her thoughts were saying she was worried the truth of what really happened would be revealed.

"Not to worry. I promise it will not hurt. Now have a seat and let's begin."

Linda did as she was told.

Nana shuffled the cards and then placed them on the table. She separated them into three piles and brought them back to one stack.

"Now, with your right-hand break into three stacks."

Linda took a deep breath before doing as she was told.

"Thank you. Now let's see what the cards have to say to us."

Nana briefly closed her eyes invoked the help of her spirit guides and all that was pure.

As Nana spread out the cards, she knew exactly what would be happening to Linda. Instead, she told her she saw a man in uniform in her future. That pleased Linda. Maybe taking the focus away from Paul would be a good thing. Although Nana saw Linda being arrested in the near future, she did not elaborate on that point as she didn't want Linda to do something drastic.

When the session was finished, Linda was so pleased she hugged Nana and thanked her for a wonderful reading. Nana reached in Linda's mind to see what was happening and was happy to see she was no longer focused on Paul. She was excited about meeting a new man, a man in uniform.

Maybe, this reading was exactly what she needed to change her future. Maybe, just maybe, if she moved away from her obsession with Paul, this "man in uniform" wouldn't happen as Nana envisioned. Maybe, he would appear in her life to help her and not to arrest her. Only time would tell. Nana hoped the reading had been enough.

After Linda had departed, Nana thanked her spirits and wrapped the tarot cards once again in the silk fabric. She cleared the table, and after she was satisfied everything was put away, she grabbed her purse and left the caravan. She had decided to wait outside in the fresh air for Bill's arrival.

Soon after Bill arrived in the golf cart. He had two grocery bags filled with food. He looked at Nana and smiled as he picked up the bags.

"You look beautiful."

Bill walked over to the picnic table and set down the bags. He proceeded to cover the picnic table with a tablecloth he produced from a separate bag. In there he had a scented candle, a silver tray, and two glasses. He whistled to himself as he placed the items on the table including the containers of food.

Once everything was set up, he removed a mini-Bluetooth speaker from the bag. He then took out his phone and Nana assumed he was looking for a playlist when all of a sudden, a melody began to play.

All during this time Nana stood transfixed.

Bill turned around and with a smile extended his hand for her to join him. He was so gallant it was hard to believe he meant any harm. Yet, as she placed her hand in his, she felt it. She knew in that instant that Bill Yardley was a dangerous man.

Protect me, she mumbled to her spirits as she sat down.

"Gracias."

"Aww, you speak Spanish. I can speak a little, but not too much."

"You don't say. You sure are full of surprises Bill Yardley."

In that instant Bill looked right at Nana. The hairs in the back of her neck raised and she felt as if he had pierced her soul. Then it was gone. Bill smiled and asked Nana if she would like some wine.

After he had served them both a glass of wine, Bill raised his glass.

"A toast!" he said, "to a new friendship."

Nana barely smiled as they clicked their glasses.

"So, tell me about yourself Nana. I'm intrigued to learn more about what makes you tick. How did you meet Juana and Eddie? Just tell me everything."

"There's not much to tell. I've known Juana and Eddie for a while. This weekend was the first time after many times of being asked, that I agreed to go with them on one of their caravan outings. Everyone I have met has been nice and welcoming."

"That's it? No! I want to know about you. What do you do, where do you live? That kind of stuff."

"Oh, I am never in any one place for long. In fact, I'm heading out to visit my granddaughter next week."

"You are?" Bill seemed to be annoyed at learning of Nana's plans.

"Yes. I often travel to wherever she is and spend a few days accompanying her. Why do you ask?"

Nana was starting to regret having agreed to lunch. She needed to know. Opening up her mind just enough to see what he was thinking was all she needed. Immediately she closed herself up and tried her best to act as if she had not learned what he was thinking.

Nana shivered at the darkness in his mind. Bill was unaware she could hear his thoughts. As he looked at her, he assumed her trembling was due to the fact that she was cold. Although why, when it was hot outside, escaped him.

"Are you alright?"

"Yes. Thank you for asking. I must be coming down with something. I haven't been feeling well lately," Nana replied, hoping he'd believe her.

It seemed to do the trick because for the remainder of lunch Bill spoke about this and that. He even told Nana how he had previously been married and was now twice a widower. He also mentioned he'd never had any children and after several years of being alone he now spent most of his time camping with the club members.

He did tell Nana at one point that he was looking for someone to spend time with and hoped there was a connection. She of course, ignored the advances and changed the subject. From all appearances Bill seemed to be a nice man who enjoyed camping with friends. But that was the persona he portrayed. Inside, there was turmoil and anger, and... something. Something that just didn't sit right with Nana.

"Hey guys, how are you both doing?"

Nana looked up to see Sally's husband Leonardo smiling at them both as if he knew a secret.

She could feel Bill's anger vibrating off of his pores. To

diffuse a potential problem, Nana smiled in return and asked Leonardo how he was doing. Bill remained silent.

"Oh, I was walking over to the food truck and noticed you both having lunch. Nice spread you guys have here," he smiled looking at Bill and Nana.

At that point Bill seemed to have composed himself, smiled, and asked him about Sally.

"She's off with some friends, I think. Haven't seen her all morning."

Nana remained silent. She was about to ask Leonardo if he wanted to join them, but thought she should not engage.

"Well, enjoy your lunch. See you both later."

As he walked away, Nana wondered about him and Sally.

"Now that he is gone, we can go back to talking about us."

"Actually, I am sorry, but I will have to cut this short. I had totally forgotten my daughter told me she was calling me in a few minutes and I don't want to miss the call. Thank you very much for a lovely lunch, Bill," she said as she stood, "let me help you pick up."

Bill did not seem happy with the turn of events, but made no effort to change her mind. After he had left, she walked into the caravan and locked the door. Nana hated to feel this way and to lie, but she felt the need to do so with Bill.

Not wanting to stay there alone, she reached out to Juana and told her she was ordering an uber. Once she confirmed they were still at the Point, she locked up the caravan and walked to the main entrance. There she ordered an uber and waited.

The driver arrived a few minutes later and off they went. By the time they got to the Point, she thanked the driver and exited the car. At the main entrance, she gave her name and was told her group was all on the back terrace. For the next few hours Nana forgot all about Bill, Linda and Sally, and the rest of the campers.

Later that evening, Juana, Eddie, and Nana headed to the

same spot where the campers had met for drinks the previous night. This time, several of the campers had set up a spread with appetizers, small bites of chicken and steak, and of course, the infamous margaritas.

She was happy. Nana realized that if she took the problem campers out of the equation, the whole idea of joining the group and getting her own caravan would be ideal.

———

The next morning, as they packed the chairs away and got ready to head home, Eddie took Nana aside and asked her how she felt about the weekend.

"I know this weekend may not have been what you expected. And, I can assure you, as I know Juana will do the same, that all of this "drama" is not common amongst our group. So, I'm hoping you have not been deterred from considering joining us in the future. I'm hoping you'll even purchase your own caravan," Eddie said with a smile.

"Do not worry. I want to assure *you* that I had a wonderful time this weekend. I am almost one hundred percent certain I'll be purchasing a caravan of my own soon."

"That is marvelous news. I'll let you tell Juana. She'll be delighted."

"I will, and again, thank you for including me this weekend. It has been amazing. Let me help you. This will be good practice for me."

For the next hour, Eddie explained to Nana what needed to be done before they could leave and she helped thinking it was something she could do on her own. When they were finished, Eddie told her she'd done a great job. Pleased with herself, she thanked him again for the millionth time and went inside to finish packing her bag.

When she exited the caravan one last time, Nana noticed several of the club members outside. She said goodbye to them and promised she'd seem them again soon. Bill at one point looked up and stared at Nana, then smiled and waved. Linda was humming to herself while she gathered her belonging. Even Sally appeared to be in good spirits.

The ride back to Juana's house was quicker than she'd expected. Before she knew it, they had arrived at the house. Nana gathered her belongings and promised Juana and Eddie, she'd let them know of her decision. Once in the truck, she called Francesca to let her know she was back.

When Francesca answered the phone, she told Nana her and Tomas were on the island. They'd wait for her at the house. Telling her daughter, she'd be there soon, she headed to the ferry. Nana was glad to be back home.

As she pulled up to her cottage, she noticed Yolanda walking outside with her overnight bag.

"Hola Yolanda, how did it go?"

"Nana, I have to tell you that I had the most wonderful and relaxing time I've had in a long time. Gracias for letting me stay here. It was exactly what I needed."

"Cuanto me alegro. I'm so glad to hear that. And the Café?"

"Ningun problema. Smooth sailing. No issues whatsoever."

"Perfecto. I'm going inside to relax for a bit, and then I'll head over to the Café later this evening. Hasta luego."

"Hasta luego Nana."

As Yolanda drove off in the direction of La Misteriosa Café, Nana smiled. She was pleased it had worked out, and was happy with the choice she'd made. Yolanda was exactly what she needed.

Once inside, Moro jumped up in circles when he saw Nana. She laughed, pleased he was so happy to see her. Francesca and Tomas stayed for a few minutes then left as they were meeting friends at the Café.

After Nana put her suitcase away, she grabbed a glass of

water and headed to the back porch. Moro followed and waited until she was ready to tell him all about her weekend.

Nana finally told him how much fun camping was and how much she had enjoyed staying in the caravan. She gave him a brief description of what happened with Sally, Linda, the argument, and even her concerns about Bill. When she was done, Moro was amazed so much drama had played out in such a short time.

So, does that mean this was your first- and last-time going camping?

"No, I'm seriously considering purchasing my own caravan. Besides the drama with those people, I did have a wonderful time."

Qué bueno. Cuanto me alegro. I'm so happy you are seriously considering this because I must tell you I'm looking forward to going camping.

Laughing Nana nodded and smiled. She closed her eyes for a few minutes and fell asleep. Moro too fell asleep. By the time, Nana woke up it had been almost two hours.

"Wow, I didn't realize how tired I was. I guess I needed that nap."

Me too.

"You always need a nap," Nana chuckled, "I'm going in to shower and head over to the Café if you want to join me."

Si, claro.

"Perfecto."

———

Two months later, Nana telephoned Juana and asked if Eddie would be available to sit down with her and help her decide on which caravan to purchase.

Juana was so excited she screamed into the phone.

"Eddie! Eddie, come here right now!"

"What? What happened?" he asked as he rushed into the room.

"Nana needs your help in picking out a caravan," she said with a huge grin on her face.

"Mujer. You are going to give me a heart attack. I thought something had happened."

"Something did happen. Nana is buying a caravan."

Shaking his head, he realized it was fruitless to try and explain to Juana that Nana buying a caravan did not constitute an emergency. So, instead he rolled his eyes before speaking.

"Juana, you know I love you right? Pero mi amor, you cannot scare me that way again. I really did think something terrible had happened."

"Perdóname. I'm sorry. I'm just so excited I couldn't help myself."

"Alright," he replied with a smile.

Juana grinned waiting for him to continue.

"Please tell Nana it will be my pleasure to help her. If she's free Saturday, we can visit a few sites that have caravans. She should be able to find something to her liking."

"Did you hear that?" Juana spoke into the receiver.

"Si, tell him thank you, and I'll see you guys on Saturday."

When the weekend rolled around, Nana realized she was more excited than she had expected. Before she left the house, she told Moro where she was going and made sure he knew that if he needed anything he just needed to reach out to her mentally. Otherwise, she'd be back soon.

She gave him a treat and left for the ferry. The trip to the mainland took less than twenty minutes. Nana arrived at Juana's house in record time. She was grateful that there was hardly any traffic. You never know in Miami what you'll find when you head out.

Eddie was outside watering the lawn when she pulled up. He waved and went to turn off the hose.

"Hola Nana. Are you ready for a new adventure?" he asked laughing.

"Sí!"

"Good. Let me tell Juana we are leaving. I'll be right back."

Within a few minutes, Eddie and Juana came outside. Juana greeted Nana with a tight hug and told her to go have fun.

"Los veo después," she said to Nana and to Eddie, she threw him a kiss.

In the car, Eddie told Nana that they would be visiting several locations. What he wanted her to do first was walk around the lot and look at the different options. He also made sure to tell her to take her time, and reminded her that she didn't even have to make a decision today. Unless she found something that called to her, today was about looking at was available in the market.

Nana was not worried. She knew that today she would purchase a caravan. It was in the cards. Her only concern was whether she'd stick to her budget or not.

As Eddie pulled up to the first location, Nana was mesmerized by the different caravans, RVs, and huge motorhomes. He turned off the ignition and looked over at Nana.

"Remember, you do not have to commit to anything today. Take your time and ask as many questions as you like. No question is wrong or silly."

Again, Nana was not worried. But she couldn't tell him she knew today was the day she'd buy her caravan or that she'd dreamt about it and even saw the one she'd buy. One thing was certain, this location was not the one with her caravan.

Instead, she smiled at Eddie and nodded. As they started to walk up to one of the motorhomes, the manager approached.

"Long time no see my friend," he said as he embraced Eddie.

"It has been a long time."

"How's the wife?"

"She's doing great. Thanks for asking. By the way, this is Rosalia."

They greeted each other and he wasted no time in pointing out a few caravans that had been reduced. He then told them he'd leave them to explore on their own. But if they needed anything he'd be in the office.

Eddie thanked him and said he'd call him soon to catch up. Once he was gone, Eddie ushered Nana toward the first motorhome.

Clearly not satisfied, they went off to see a few caravans. After a while Nana stopped.

"Eddie, I don't see anything here that grabs my attention. You mentioned there were a few more locations we could visit?"

"Yes. Let's go to the next place I have in mind. This location we are going to next, so that you know, has older models. Some are new and some are used caravans. If you don't like anything there, then I have one more spot we can visit."

"Perfecto. I have a good feeling I'm going to find just what I'm looking for before the end of the day," Nana said with a smile.

After looking around and not finding anything to her liking they drove into the next lot. Nana's fingers began to tingle. She knew this was where she'd find her caravan. She was so excited she could hardly wait to get out of the car. At first, she didn't see the caravan and was going through the motions until they walked to the end of the lot. Far in the corner was a caravan that had seen better days. She turned to Eddie and pointed.

"What about that one?"

"That caravan? I'm not sure you should consider that one. It seems to have seen better days."

Nana chuckled as she realized that to him it looked like it was not worth it. To her, it was perfect.

"Ese es el que yo quiero. I want that one."

Eddie looked at Nana for a split second before shrugging his shoulders.

"Alright, let me get someone to help us."

As Eddie walked away Nana stood in place. She dared not approach the caravan until they returned. When the man next to her spoke, she was startled.

"I'm sorry, I didn't mean to startle you."

He was a stocky middle-aged man wearing a suit too small for his body. Nana tried not to look at him in case she couldn't control herself.

"No, that's alright. What can you tell me about that caravan?"

The man was salivating. Nana immediately entered his mind and found out why.

If I can finally get rid of this caravan that will be wonderful. If she doesn't bite, then I'm dropping it off at the junk yard. That caravan has been nothing but trouble since the moment it arrived on the lot. No one can keep it more than a few days without returning it. Some nonsense about things moving around and cold spots inside. All I need is to convince her this caravan was meant for her.

"So, this is a beauty. You have a very good eye," he said with a smile."

"How much?"

"Nana, wait you haven't even looked inside."

Turning to Eddie she patted his arm and told him not to worry.

"So, how much?" she said as she turned to the salesman.

When he gave her a price it was way lower than she'd expected. Before she could answer Eddie said he needed to speak with her in private.

"Nana, that price is unusually low for this type of caravan. I'm certain there is something wrong with it. You really should keep looking."

"Eddie, don't worry. This is the caravan I want, and the fact that the price is so low … it's perfect," she said with a smile and walked back to the salesman.

"You have yourself a deal."

Let's hope she doesn't come back in a few days to tell me she wants to return it.

They walked to the office in silence. Nana and Eddie looked over the contract, and he again cautioned her about buying the caravan unseen. She assured him she knew exactly what she was doing. One thing she did ask Eddie before she signed was where they could take it to be remodeled. If he didn't have a suitable place, she might have to decline the offer.

He informed her that he had someone and once everything was settled, they would pick up caravan and take it back to their shop for the remodeling.

Delighted, Nana signed the contract, gave them a check and was given the keys to her new vintage caravan. Once she had her keys in her hand she turned to Eddie.

"Alright, it's time to call your guy to pick up my new baby," she said with a smile.

Once Eddie finished the call, they confirmed with the salesperson that someone would stop by the following day to pick it up. Thrilled, he was willing to agree to just about anything as long as they took it off the lot.

As they left, Eddie was thinking Nana had lost her marbles. She in turn chuckled.

When they arrived at the house Juana came out running.

"Well? Did you find anything you liked? Should I go with you next time to help you decide?"

Eddie shook his head back and forth and raised his hands in the air as he walked up to Juana.

"Esta mujer has purchased a vintage, mind you, a vintage caravan that looks like it's about to fall apart. I tried to warn her, but she ignored my advice."

"Don't mind him. Tell me everything," Juana said to Nana.

"Eddie is correct. It has seen better days, but I'm certain once I've had it remodeled and painted it'll be like new."

"Que bueno! I'm so happy. You are now officially a camper."

"Si. Anyway, I have to head home. Eddie's friend is picking it up in a few days and taking it to his shop to begin the remodeling. He said he'd call me when they were ready for me to come by and tell them what I want. When they do call, do you want to come with me? I could always use a second pair of eyes."

"Por supuesto. ¡Claro que sí!"

"Perfecto. See you later."

Juana waited until Nana had driven away before heading inside.

"Eddie!"

"Coming."

"What happened?"

"Nothing bad. She just decided on purchasing a caravan that was definitely vintage and without even going inside. She said she knew the moment she laid eyes on it, that it was the caravan she was meant to have. I don't understand it, but the price was so low I couldn't see myself trying to talk her out of it. Although, I doubt it would have made a difference. She was determined to purchase that particular caravan."

"Interesting. I'm sure she saw something or felt something that told her she needed to buy that caravan. I can't wait to see it."

"Well, don't expect much. Trust me, it looks like it is not even livable. I was surprised it was even in the lot."

"Well, maybe it was waiting for her. Anyway, she's asked

me to accompany her to the shop when they call her. Will that be alright with you?"

"Si mi vida. Claro."

"Wonderful."

Four months later, Nana was the proud owner of a newly renovated caravan.

❖

———

❖

Chapter 3

❖

N ana's newly remodeled vintage caravan was equipped with a mini fridge, a sink, a shower head, a small toilet, and a few cabinets. They even installed a couch that could be flattened out and converted to a table. The chairs were included in the design so all she had to do was remove the clip and slide out the chairs.

The walls were painted a light sage, and included white shelves. She even added a few extra light fixtures and hung a string of lights over her bed for ambiance. There were enough storage nooks for all of her essentials including a place to store her food, clothing, and shoes. Nana was amazed how they were able to utilize every inch of the caravan and it didn't look cramped at all. In fact, it looked very cozy.

As a final touch, she had decorated the bed with a rich turquoise duvet cover, that had accents of gold and midnight blue. The drapes reached just to the bottom of the window sill and were white linen with a touch of lace.

Every inch of wood had some form of carving. She had been surprised that this caravan had sat on the lot for so long without anyone purchasing it. The details were stunning. It felt homey and cozy, just what she needed.

As she looked around the caravan she noticed to the side of the bed, closer to the floor, there was a panel.

Not having noticed it before, she bent down and tapped on it. Nothing happened. Then she thought if she pushed it, it may reveal a hidden area. She couldn't recall telling them to install this panel, but thought maybe they had wanted to surprise her with an extra feature.

She tried again and still nothing happened. *That's strange*, she thought to herself. Why put a panel which appears can be opened, to then not have it open at all, strange indeed.

Then as if someone had whispered in her ear it came to her… if she tapped on the four corners and the symbol in the center, maybe that would do the trick.

Nana looked around and didn't see anyone. No ghost. She followed her instinct, and sure enough, as she pushed the panel it popped open. What she found inside was something she wasn't expecting to find. There wrapped in a piece of fabric was a crystal ball.

She thought back when she first inspected the caravan and couldn't remember seeing the hidden panel, let alone hearing anything about a crystal ball.

That was very strange, she thought to herself.

As she reached out to pick up the crystal ball, she felt a tingle run up her arm. But not only that, she also could've sworn it hummed. She pulled her hand back and was about to close the panel door, until she could figure out what to do with the crystal ball, when she heard a voice.

"So, it's about time you found it," the raspy voice of a woman said.

Nana jumped so high she knocked her head on the light fixture.

"Ouch! Who are you?" she asked.

"I'm Matilda, and this here is my caravan. I can't believe

you can see me!" she was elated to finally be in the presence of someone who could actually see her.

"I'm Rosalia Gomez, but everyone calls me Nana," she replied.

"Huh, I see you've remodeled?" she said looking around more closely.

"Si, it was in need of a new look. So, I had it completely remodeled. Now, that I see you standing there almost fading I realize your predicament. I should have known this was not going to be as smooth as I had anticipated," Nana replied arching her eyebrows.

"Well, you've done a great job with the place. What's most important to me is you. I have been waiting for someone to touch my crystal ball in order to bring me back to life," Matilda kept looking around the caravan as she spoke.

"You do realize you're not really alive right? You're just a ghost," Nana tried to tell her.

"Semantics. Besides the fact that you can see me, that's all I need. It's been, wait I can't even remember how long it's been since I've spoken to a human being?" Matilda looked confused.

"Rauuul!" Nana yelled.

Immediately, Raul popped in.

"What is so urgent you had to scream for me? If you must know I was walking the streets of Paris when you scared the heck out of me," Raul said as he placed his hands on his translucent hips.

Before Nana could respond he looked over at Matilda and whistled.

"Who do we have here? Hay Dios Mio mama," Raul smiled.

"Don't hay mama me. That isn't helpful. Yes, she's beautiful. The problem we have here is ... apparently, I've awakened her by touching her crystal ball," Nana sounded frustrated.

Pointing to Matilda she continued.

"See if you can please, figure out a way to get rid of her," Nana expected Raul to figure out a solution.

"Let me see what I can find out," Raul said as he floated over to Matilda who was in the far corner trying to grab one of the pillows on the bed.

Raul looked over at Nana who just shrugged. Clearing his throat, he tried to get her attention.

"Excuse me, I'm Raul Silva. I'm a friend of Nana. I wanted to see if I could help you move on. You probably miss your family?" he spoke softly.

Turning around she looked directly into his eyes.

"No thank you. This is my home and I'm not going anywhere. Based on my family laws, I don't have to go if I don't want to, and I choose to stay," she smiled and turned back around.

Floating back to Nana he whispered.

"You have a problem," Raul said with a frown.

"Really? You think?" she answered sarcastically.

"She's Romani, which means she's not going anywhere. If you keep this vintage caravan then she's part of the package. Sorry, but there's nothing I can do if she doesn't want to move on," he shrugged his shoulders.

"Por Dios. Ugh, fine go back to Paris. Tell Rosa I love her. And, as to this one, I'll find a way of dealing with her," Nana said as she nodded towards Matilda.

After Raul had disappeared, Nana closed her eyes for a second before she spoke.

"Matilda, it appears we got off on the wrong foot," she said as she looked more closely at her.

As Nana focused on her features, she could tell she was of gypsy descent. She had the skirt, the ruffled shirt, the shawl wrapped around her shoulders, and the bandanna on her forehead. She was quite stunning with that long brownish hair and deep piercing green eyes.

Yup, she's gypsy, Nana thought to herself.

Matilda appeared to be in her mid-thirties. She wondered though when she died and what was the cause of death, but she figured that would come with time. If she couldn't get rid of her, then she needed to make the best of the situation.

"No problem. I see you're planning a trip. Where we going?" she asked.

Just then Moro entered the caravan and barked. Matilda shrieked and disappeared.

Well, that's one way of getting rid of her, Nana thought to herself as she chuckled.

N ana had previously made special arrangements with Colten Island to allow her to store her caravan at the side of her cottage. Since the area where her house was located had lots of trees keeping the caravan in the back and away from prying eyes was perfect.

Preparations for her long-awaited vacation were underway. Yolanda would move into the cottage for the next year. Francesca and Tomas would stop by at least once a week to make certain everything was running smoothly.

The time was fast arriving when Nana would head out with the Miami Coastal Caravan Club members on her very first solo trip. Everything was set. The caravan was fully stocked, her clothes and food had been put away. All of Moro's toys and treats were in the cabinet, and his dry food was stored away in his special compartment. Nana was set to meet at Juana and Eddie's house in about an hour.

Matilda had not made her presence known since Moro scared her away. So, Nana hoped she wouldn't be a problem once they hit the road.

Nana contacted the ferry manager to inform him that she would be taking her caravan on the noon ferry. Once confirmed, she checked the house again, and locked it before heading to the Café. Although she normally would not lock her cottage, she felt more comfortable if Yolanda kept it locked when she was either at the Café or off the island.

As she walked into La Misteriosa Café every single one of her staff members congratulated her on her upcoming trip. Some of the regular customers even offered her well wishes and bon voyage. Satisfied everything was in order she got into her truck and headed towards the ferry with Moro in tow.

Just as she arrived to get in line, she saw Francesca and Tomas were waiting by the side of the ferry.

"You didn't think you'd leave without saying goodbye right?"

"Hay que bueno. I'm so glad you guys made it. I know how busy you were this morning and I didn't want to be an imposition."

"Por favor Mami. How could you say that? We'd never let you leave without saying goodbye."

"You're too sweet. Gracias."

After a few minutes Nana was ready to hand over the reins of the caravan to one of the guards on duty. One thing she was still not accustomed to was driving that thing onto the ferry. She had practiced several times and knew the truck she had purchased would do the job without making her feel she had no control.

Nana hugged Francesca again tightly and kissed her, promising she'd call often. She then kissed and hugged Tomas and waved goodbye as she and Moro walked onto the ferry. As it sailed away, she waved for the last time as a teardrop trickled down her cheek. She knew this was what she needed, but she also knew it was going to be hard being away from family for so long.

Moro barked to get her attention.

Don't be sad Nana. It's going to be fine and we'll be back before you know it.

Looking down at Moro she smiled and nodded.

Less than twenty minutes later they had arrived on the mainland. The guard was nice enough to drive it for her off the ferry and station it where she could easily drive it off the lot.

"Alright, here we go."

To new adventures, to chasing squirrels, to …

Moro was so excited he couldn't finish his thought. Laughing she patted him on the head and turned on the music. Her playlist choice today was 1980s music. She knew most of the tunes, and as she sang along Moro bobbed his head.

Matilda had kept her distance since Moro startled her previously. She also wanted to observe how Nana behaved around her caravan. When she learned that she could see and also speak with ghosts, and that she was a whiz in tarot card reading, she was intrigued.

Pulling up to Juana's house she noticed their caravan door open. Nana parked and turned off the ignition of her truck. Before walking out she reminded Moro to behave as she was letting him out without a leash.

"Come on, it's officially the beginning of our vacation."

Moro barked as he jumped out of the truck.

Once he had run around in circles a few times, he sniffed around the grass looking for a place to mark his territory. Approaching the door of the caravan, Nana realized no one was inside. She turned and walked to the front door. As she rang the doorbell, she smiled at Moro who had found a spot under the big cypress tree.

Juana opened the door and yelled out *"she's here"* to her husband.

"Just letting Eddie know you've arrived. I have to finish

up a few things and then we can leave. Here, follow me to the caravan as I put my suitcase away."

Nana followed, as did Moro.

"So, the plan is to meet up with everyone at the first stop on the Turnpike. That would be by exit 4. Once everyone is there then we'll form a line with Bill being the leader. You can follow us the entire way so that if you need anything you can either honk at Eddie or flash your lights."

"Sounds like a plan."

"As a matter of fact, it just occurred to me ... do you want me to ride with you in your truck?"

"No," she yelled at the same time Moro barked.

"Wow, I only thought it might make you feel less nervous if I rode with you, but no worries."

"Juana, perdóname. It's not that at all. I just realized I forgot one of Moro's toys. It's no big deal. Sorry. No need for you to ride with me, I'm confident everything will be fine."

The last thing Nana needed was for Juana to feel a cold draft or see something moving in the truck. Even though Matilda had been missing in action, she didn't trust that she wouldn't appear any moment, and she was in no mood to explain to Juana about her newly acquired resident ghost.

"Bueno, if you change your mind, we can make the change at the next stop. Once we hit the road we usually do not stop until we've been driving for about four hours. Make sure you go to the restroom and get anything you need out of your caravan before we start the trip. I need to go back inside. You are more than welcome to follow me or wait here."

"Ningun problema, I'll just wait here."

"Alright, see you in a bit."

Juana walked back into her house as Eddie walked out. He approached Nana, greeted her, and asked if there was anything he could do to help.

"No, gracias. I think I have everything under control. Juana already told me I could always flash the lights or honk if I need you guys once we're on the road, but I'm confident there will be no problem that can't wait until our next stop."

"Esta bien, if you change your mind just let me know."

Eddie went off to check on a few things and left Nana standing there with Moro. At that moment Matilda had manifested and was watching them from inside the caravan. She was happy they were finally taking her baby on the road. If only she could remember how she ended up a ghost. That would explain a lot of the things that were still fuzzy.

A short time later, Juana and Eddie came out of the house, locked the door and told Nana to gear up, they were ready to roll.

"Did Juana explain where we are going first?" Eddie asked.

"Si, gracias. She told me we are meeting the rest of the club members at the rest stop on exit 4."

"Yes. Good. Alright you can follow us and stay behind us at all times. However, if for any reason we are separated just meet us at the stop."

"Sounds like a plan. See you soon."

Nana waved as she walked over to her truck, got inside and started the engine. Moro settled in the backseat with one of his toys while Nana took several deep breaths before starting the engine.

The drive to the Turnpike was easy. The scary part was entering the highway while driving a truck that had a caravan attached to it. Surprisingly she was able to enter the highway easily. After driving for a few minutes, Nana started to relax thinking to herself that this was going to be a breeze.

Just as she was adjusting the radio Matilda appeared.

"Stop!"

Nana slammed on the brakes as she swerved off the road. Immediately, her phone rang.

"Nana, are you alright? ¿Te pasó algo?"

"Perdóname. I didn't mean to startle you. I just turned the

wheel quicker than I expected. Everything is fine," she said looking at Matilda with narrow eyes.

"Well then, alright. Talk soon," Juana said, and with that hung up the phone.

Focusing back on the issue at hand, Nana took a deep breath before she spoke.

"Now let me tell you something *Matilda*," she yelled out into the ether. You may have been the previous owner of this caravan, but it doesn't give you the right to pop in whenever you want, and especially yell at me like you did a minute ago. Estamos claro?" Nana yelled.

"Is that necessary? I may be dead, but I'm not deaf," Matilda responded, appearing in the seat next to Nana.

"Would you like to explain to me why you screamed?" Nana asked.

"Why bother?" Matilda sat there annoyed at Nana.

Taking a deep breath, Nana tried again.

"Can you please tell me why you screamed for me to stop?"

"I could see that up ahead the first caravan hit a deer. If you didn't suddenly stop, you'd be involved in a pileup. I was trying to save your life."

The fact was that Nana had slammed on the brakes making Eddie also slowdown, which then allowed them both the opportunity to avoid being involved in a collision.

Nana felt ashamed that she had screamed at Matilda. In that instant Eddie put the right signal on started to slowly move onto the side of the road. Nana followed until she came to a full stop.

"I'm sorry. It's just you scared me. I do appreciate you warning me, maybe next time you can tell me and not scream?" Nana smiled at Matilda in hopes she'd not take offense.

Matilda didn't say anything at first, then just as she was

about to respond, Eddie walked up to the driver side window. She took that opportunity to disappear.

"Nana are you alright?"

"Yes. What happened?"

"I just received a call letting me know the first caravan apparently hit a deer. There's a pileup and the two of us are very lucky because with you swerving off the road and me noticing it and slowing down, we were able to avoid hitting any of the people in front of us."

"Dios Mio. Is anyone hurt?"

"I'm not sure. If you are certain you're alright, I'll go check and let you know."

"Yes, of course. If you need any help, let me know."

Eddie waved at the rest of the caravans behind Nana. They all stuck their hands out the window with a thumbs up indicating everyone was doing alright. Eddie walked away feeling very lucky that no one else had been hurt.

However, as he walked back to and past his caravan, he realized the extent of the pile up and it didn't look good. After the police and ambulance arrived and took several of the club members to the local hospital, it was agreed that they could park in the far end of the hospital overnight. The lot had just been paved and was not yet in use.

Once everyone was settled in, Bill, the president of the club, went to each member to let them know they'd be setting up a temporary table by his RV so that anyone who wanted to stop by and chat or hang out could do so.

Everyone wanted to stay close. So, after they had all ordered their meals, it was agreed that Eddie and Bill would go pick up the food. Juana stopped by for a few minutes to make sure Nana was doing alright, and then headed back to her caravan. She said she wanted to lay down for a little bit.

Matilda appeared just as Nana was about to sit down.

"Hello," she whispered.

"Que cómica. You are very funny Matilda." Nana replied.

"I wouldn't want to *startle* you," she replied with sarcasm.

Nana looked at her and didn't reply. She realized it was fruitless to continue to nag her so she changed tactics.

"How are you feeling?"

"I'm more shook up than I realized. Thank you again for warning me. You may have just saved my life," Nana replied.

"So, I saved your life," Matilda said with a smile.

Oh boy, great. Nana thought to herself. Now she was in trouble.

Matilda waltzed around the caravan. *Guess that's how she got the name Waltzing Matilda,* Nana thought to herself and laughed.

"I'm going to lay down for a few minutes," she said as she took off her shoes and placed them in the cupboard.

"You do that, I'll be back shortly."

And with that poof, she disappeared again.

Later feeling somewhat refreshed Nana changed out of her travel cloths and put on some jeans and a fresh shirt. Looking at herself in the mirror to make sure she looked good she smiled and then left the caravan with Moro in tow.

She was rather hesitant as she walked over to Bill's RV. When they'd originally started out, she hadn't noticed he was the last RV in the convoy, and since as she had not seen him since their lunch date, she felt their encounter might be awkward. He had called incessantly every day for over a month, and then finally had given up when it became evident that Nana was not interested.

Acting as if she had not seen him, Nana greeted the club members until she had no choice but to say hello.

"Well, well. What do we have here? You're alive," he said with sarcasm in his voice.

"Bill. How are you?"

"I'm doing well Nana. It seems you are too."

"Yes, well, I'm looking forward to this trip," she said,

thinking she wasn't at all sure if she could handle being around Bill for a full year.

"I'm sure we'll have plenty of time to catch up."

"Great," she replied thinking desperate times meant desperate measures.

It was time to bring in reinforcements. Later she'd devise a plan that would ensure Bill left her alone the remainder of the trip. For now, she would enjoy seeing everyone again and focus instead on the drive north.

By the time everyone had checked-in, Nana had spoken to those she knew and introduced herself to members she had not previously met. Eddie walked up to the group and let them know that thankfully no one had any life-threatening injuries, and that based on what the doctors said, the rest of the campers would be able to leave first thing in the morning.

The roar of the engines in the morning had Nana scrambling to get out of bed. For some reason the alarm never sounded so now she was frantic to put everything away that could be knocked down. When she was finished, she stepped out of her caravan to find most of the members had gathered outside Eddie and Juana's spot.

"For those that want to follow us, we will leave in an hour. We are going to breakfast now at the IHop next door. Bill is assisting those that cannot travel with us any longer and will return shortly before we're ready to go."

Nana nodded at Eddie and went back inside her caravan to grab her purse. During breakfast, the group discussed what had happened. Eddie was the only one that mentioned having slowed down because he noticed Nana's truck buckle as if she had put her foot on the brake making her caravan sway from side to side.

Everyone was grateful for the sudden stop because they too had been able to avoid the collision. Once they returned to their respective trucks no one spoke. They all went about their business and by the time Bill arrived they were all sitting in their trucks.

For the next several days the Miami Coastal Caravan Club traveled as a convoy on their course to their final destination, Vermont, stopping along the way several times to rest.

———

Crystal Falls Campground was now less than two miles away. The day had finally arrived and Nana was excited to park the caravan in its final resting place for more than a few hours. For the most part, Matilda had kept her distance, appearing only a few times to annoy her and Moro, or to talk incessantly about her life when she was alive.

When it became evident, they were not going to play her game, she'd disappear in a puff. That was fine with Nana who still had not figured out how to get rid of her.

Crystal Falls belonged to a dear friend of Eddie. It sat on forty-two acres of private land. Surrounded by plush trees, a newly built main house where guests could gather by the fireplace, have drinks at the bar, take a dip in the hot tub, or even hang out in the game room. It sounded like paradise. It had everything you'd want in an adult campground.

She had been warned that there were no signs indicating it was an actual campground. Only a small post that read "Valdez" at the beginning of the drive. That was the only indication there was anything at all down the long dirt road. A road that was a mile long and hidden from plain sight. It was the ideal getaway for anyone who wanted privacy.

Valdez who had grown up next door to Eddie before moving to the area had done so when he inherited the land from his grandfather. Recently, he had begun to open up the area to paying guests. Although he maintained an open policy for friends and family letting them know they would always have a free place to park, he thought why not mix it up a bit.

This was on a trial basis, but if everything went the way he'd hoped, he would be able to sustain both sides successfully. The area for family and friends was the one that you had to know was down the dirt road. The one for paying guests was accessible through a gate at the far end of the forty-two acres. Valdez had purposely kept undeveloped land in between the two areas so as not to have anyone accidentally walk in to the wrong side.

Valdez had also built a main house that was large enough to accommodate over fifty people at one time.

One by one, the Miami Coastal Caravan members drove down the dirt road following the signs to their respective spaces. Each member had been given a map and a slot number where they could park their caravans or motor homes for the duration of their stay. Everything had been set up where all they had to do was park, plug everything in, and sit back and relax.

Valdez had taken the extra step this year to hire additional help that would be available to the club members in case they needed anything in particular.

Once everyone had settled in, Olga, Valdez' assistant, greeted each member individually letting them know Valdez would stop by later that evening to say hello. However, for now she was there to answer any questions and to provide them a list of all the new amenities, and a few surprises that had been set up just for them.

"Well, Moro, estamos aquí. Now that we're here, remember not to wander too far. Be careful exploring the surrounding area."

No te preocupes. I'll stay close.

"Good. Have fun," Nana said to Moro with a smile.

As she stepped out of her caravan, she noticed all the

other club members setting up and securing their spaces. Bill suddenly appeared next to her. Startled, she jumped.

"Oh, so sorry Nana. I didn't mean to startle you," Bill said looking intently at her.

"No, it's fine. Ningún problema."

"Well, I just stopped by to see if there was anything you needed."

"No, gracias. I'm all set," she answered as she turned around.

Realizing she was not going to engage in idle conversation, Bill turned around and walked away. *Again, with the anger. What is his problem*? she thought to herself as she busied herself.

Nana decided it was time to talk to Juana and Eddie. She'd find a time within the next few days to ask them about him. If she didn't nip this in the bud right away, she'd find herself in a sticky situation and that was the last thing she wanted.

Woo hoo.

Nana looked up to see Matilda at the window. Closing her eyes, she tried her best to ignore her. That didn't work. The caravan started to shake from side to side. Several of the club members stopped what they were doing in disbelief.

Great. I'm going to kill her.

Taking a deep breath, Nana stopped what she was doing and entered the caravan as it stopped shaking.

"Matilda, always a pleasure to see you. What do you want?"

Well, you don't have to get snippy.

"Again, what can I do for you Matilda? As you can see, I'm quite busy."

You need to start using the crystal ball. It's been calling out to you and ignoring it is not going to make it go away. Besides, there is danger afoot and you need to prepare yourself for what's coming.

"First of all, I have never used a crystal ball and have no

intention of starting now. And, what do you mean about danger coming? Wait, the pile-up was not enough? You are now telling me that something else is going to happen?" Nana asked trying not to sound concerned.

That perpetual humming you have tried to ignore is speaking to you. It's telling you, it's ready. You need to take ownership and start using it or you'll go raving mad.

"What do you mean I'll go raving mad? What are you talking about?"

Well, not really raving mad. Here's the thing. That humming sound is driving me crazy and you need to make it stop.

"And, why again is this my problem?"

Do I have to spell it out to you?

"Apparently yes you do. So, start from the beginning," Nana said as she sat down. She patiently waited until Matilda was ready to start speaking.

Having been left with no choice, Matilda paced around the caravan several times before she began her story. By the time she had finished, Nana had learned that Matilda had been cursed at the time of her death. And, part of that curse was the nonstop humming of the crystal ball.

Eventually, Matilda learned that if the right person had the "gift" and would start using the crystal ball, the humming would stop. It had been so long since someone as powerful as Nana had owned the caravan that Matilda was certain she was the answer she'd been looking for all this time. She waited in anticipation for Nana's response.

"I don't know what to say," Nana was torn.

That humming was rather annoying, and maybe she could cut a deal with Matilda to stay away if she promised to use the crystal ball.

Say you'll help me; in turn I will help you.

"Let me think about it. So, you know, I do feel bad for what happened to you. But for now, I must go take care of securing the caravan and then we're all meeting afterwards.

As I said, let me think about it and I'll get back to you," Nana said as she stood.

Fine, Matilda said as she faded away.

For the next hour Nana prepared the caravan for the long stay, emptied her suitcase, replenished the fridge and set up the outside just the way she liked it. In the distance, Nana could see Moro running around a tree. Happy he was behaving she sat down in one of the chairs and thought about everything Matilda had told her.

Nana noticed an RV drive past her space. It seemed to her it might be the same RV that Sally had climbed into that weekend when she thought no one had seen her. Very interesting. Maybe this time she'd have a chance to meet the mysterious driver.

By late afternoon all of the camper's friends and guests alike had gathered behind the Main House where they had set up several fire pits. In one corner there was a table where you could pick up what you needed to make smores. Another table had sweets, and on the opposite side of the room was the bartender. After they all had what they needed, each took a seat around one of the fire pits.

Several of the club members waved as a tall handsome man accompanied by a slender black hair blue eyed woman exited a golf cart.

"Hello everyone. Bienvenido. I wanted to take this opportunity to welcome old friends and introduce myself to those who do not know me. I'm Valdez, owner of this here establishment, and this," he pointed to the woman next to him, "is Olga my assistant."

As he continued to speak, Olga handed out an activity sheet so all could see what they had organized for the remainder of the month.

"For those of you on the extended stay program, every month we will post in the lobby of the main house that month's activities. Tonight, we are offering hot cider, hot chocolate, and a few other surprises. Those can be found through those doors that lead into the sitting room. Thank you again for spending your time here at Crystal Falls."

Valdez went around and greeted the newcomers first and then headed to the side where the Miami Coastal Caravan Club members had congregated.

"Valdez, how's it going?"

"Hey, Eddie. I'm glad to see you. It's been too long," he said as he hugged him.

"Thanks for having us, man. We are all excited to spend the next year here surrounded by all of this beauty," Eddie said with a smile.

"Well, mi casa is your casa."

Valdez stayed for a while catching up with everyone and then bid the group goodnight. By the time Nana went to bed, she and Moro were so tired she couldn't see straight. She could've sworn she heard Matilda calling out her name before she gave into exhaustion.

As she drifted off, she fell into a dream …

She could hear him gasping for air. He was trying to call out a name. That voice, it was familiar to her, but she couldn't place it.

Then the scene changed and she was in the woods. He had caught up to her and now had his hands around her neck. As he squeezed her throat tighter, he got close to her ear and whispered.

"I've been waiting for you. Did you really think you could get rid of me that easily?"

At this point she had lost all hope of surviving. Although she tried, it was useless. He had drugged her and she didn't have enough strength to fight back.

As the light went out from her eyes, she saw Matilda reminding her she'd been warned.

Nana woke up gasping, her entire body shaking. Moro sat up and barked. He knew something had happened in her sleep. He barked again.

Are you alright?

"Yes, Moro. It was just a bad dream."

She looked worried, and Moro knew she was not being honest with him.

"We'll talk about it in the morning. For now, let's try to go back to sleep."

Are you certain everything is alright? You were gasping and yelling out … I've never seen you this way.

"Everything is going to be fine," Nana responded, and turned the light off and closed her eyes.

During this time, Matilda was standing in the corner hidden in the shadows. She wondered if she should tell her what she'd seen. Maybe best to keep out of it. Satisfied Nana was not in any immediate danger, she vanished, promising to herself she'd return in the morning.

At the same time Nana had been having a nightmare, Leonardo had opened his eyes and reached over to the other side of the bed hoping she was there, but as expected it was empty. He couldn't understand why she insisted on coming on these trips when she spent most of the time away from him.

October in Vermont was his favorite time of the year, and he had made a conscious decision that on this trip he would not let Sally's disappearances ruin it for him.

After taking a deep breath and stretching, Leonardo hauled himself out of bed. Their RV, one of the largest, had been the first gift he bought himself after receiving his inheritance. It turned out, a distant uncle he didn't even know existed, had left him quite a large sum of money. It was enough to allow him to buy the mobile home and invest the rest.

Leonardo was so good at investments that in less than two years he had more than tripled his earnings. No one knew he was quite the wealthy man, not even Sally.

His favorite area of the mobile home was the kitchen

where they had top of the line appliances, and enough gadgets to make a chef salivate.

These days he cooked for himself and every morning like clockwork made the coffee. Sally sometimes made a meal, but for the most part he was the chef of the house. Either that or starve, his choice.

Now that they had arrived in Vermont, he had been looking forward to everything the campground had to offer. Leonardo hoped this would bring Sally and him closer again. He just had to figure out a way to make that happen.

Looking out the window, he saw Sally sitting around the campfire with a few other campers. Not wanting to cause an argument, he returned to the kitchen and boiled some water. Chamomile tea always helped him fall asleep.

Two campers away, Linda and her new beau were debating a recent movie they had watched. She seemed happy, but in the back of her mind she wondered if he would betray her just like her old boyfriend. This time however, if that happened, she would make sure it was the last time anything like that happened to her. She would not tolerate being betrayed.

"Penny for your thoughts?"

"Oh, sorry. I was just thinking I'm the luckiest woman in the world to have met you," Linda said with a smile."

"I'm the lucky one. Now come here," he responded as he grabbed her and kissed her passionately.

While Linda and her beau were carousing in their caravan, Sally was enjoying her time outside. Having forgotten all about Leonardo, she urged some of the campers to get up and dance with her. That party continued for another few hours before everyone said their goodnights.

Reluctantly, Sally returned to her RV hoping to find Leonardo sleeping. She was in no mood to speak with him. Sure enough, as she opened the door quietly, she could hear him snoring.

Good, he must have been sleeping all this time. He'll think I've been here all night long.

As Sally crawled into bed, Leonardo had been facing away from her. In fact, he wasn't even sleeping. He knew how to fake a snore, and that was exactly what he had been doing when Sally sneaked into bed.

Leonardo knew exactly at what time Sally had come home. His anger built as he realized she hadn't even bothered to wash off the smell of aftershave. He became infuriated with her lack of respect. He would never be so blatant. Falling back asleep he reminded himself that soon, all of this would be a thing of the past.

❖

———

❖

Chapter 4

T he next morning, Nana awoke earlier than usual. Moro was sleeping in the corner and Matilda was trying to grab the crystal ball. All Nana could do at the sight of Matilda was laugh.

She did wonder though, if she should indulge her and use the crystal ball as she had suggested or figure out another way of keeping her at bay. Before she could think about it any further, she heard a blood curdling scream loud enough to wake half of Vermont.

Nana ran to the door and opened it to see Sally standing outside her RV screaming. She then staggered a bit and grabbed onto the lounge chair next to her for support.

Returning inside to grab her bathrobe, Nana ran back outside, Moro in tow. She was the first one to reach Sally.

"What's wrong Sally? What happened?"

Sally just stood there continuing to scream.

"Take a deep breath and tell me what happened," Nana placed her hand on her shoulder and gently guided her to the chair.

Focusing, Sally sat down and opened her mouth to speak, but nothing came out.

"Sally, look directly at me. Now close your eyes and take a deep breath."

Sally did as she was told and then pointed to her RV. At this point a few of the other campers had gathered around unsure of what to do. Nana turned around and spoke to the group.

"Juana, stay with Sally. The rest of you wait here while I go inside."

The door was already ajar, so Nana moved it with her foot as to not leave fingerprints and peaked inside. She could see Leonardo laying on the floor. He was not moving.

As she approached the body, she knew immediately he was dead. Not wanting to compromise the scene, she placed two fingers on his neck. She needed to ensure he was indeed dead before calling the police.

Nana stood and looked around to see if there were any clues or anything that could help her figure out what happened.

From what she could gather, Leonardo was in a fetal position undressed with only a towel partially covering his waist. The expression on his face was of pain.

Could he have come out of the shower and fallen to his death just outside the bathroom? Looking around she was amazed at the inside of the RV. This was her first time inside this RV and boy, was she surprised at how extravagant everything looked.

She inched her way towards what she believed to be the bathroom and using her sleeve opened the door. *Interesting,* she thought to herself. *It was dry as a bone.* Continuing her search she looked in the bedroom and throughout the various other rooms. Nothing seemed obviously out of place to her.

Returning to the body she wondered if it was simply a heart attack. Then she remembered the previous night one of the guests had said a masseuse would be stopping by in the morning. He would be available for anyone that wanted an hour session.

She wondered if Leonardo was getting ready for a massage when this had happened. Nana needed to find out more before she could ascertain if this was an accident or something else. But the one thing that she found interesting was where Sally had been all this time. Why did she only just find him now?

These were questions she needed answered. For now, Nana was confident there was nothing else she could do except wait for the local authorities. Looking around one more time she walked toward the door and out of the RV.

Despite it being early in the morning, a crowd had already formed.

Eddie was the first one to speak.

"What happened?"

"Leonardo is dead," Nana responded, looking at everyone that had gathered around the RV.

"I'll call 911 while you," Juana said as she pointed to Linda, "run and get Valdez or Olga, whomever is available.

Turning to Sally once again, Nana asked what had happened.

"I don't know! I walked inside and he was there on the floor. I called out to him over and over again, and when I realized he was not moving I ran outside."

"Did he have a heart problem?"

"No, he was healthy as an ox."

"Perhaps he had a massage scheduled for this morning?" Nana watched her reaction.

A small twitch appeared on her face that would have been missed if she was not looking for it.

"Oh, yes. That must be it. He was having a massage."

"That would explain why he was only wearing a towel.

But I didn't see anyone else or the massage table. Do you know at what time he had his massage?"

"No. I just came into the RV and saw him there on the floor," she responded, and as if on cue, started crying.

Nana found it odd that she found him like that because that meant she'd not been in the RV. The question would be whether she'd been gone all morning and if so, where had she been? Or had she even slept in the RV? Those questions she'd reserve for later.

Looking around the group Nana asked if anyone had seen the masseuse?

A man standing in the crowd pointed to the RV behind him. Nana walked up to him.

"Hi, I'm Nana, and you are?"

"My name is Roger Thompson. I believe he is in Mario's RV," he said as he pointed again to the caravan behind him.

"Thank you."

Nana recognized the RV as the one Sally had entered that weekend in Marathon. The mysterious man, she said to herself as she walked over to the RV and knocked. After a few seconds the door was opened by a burly man wearing a white uniform.

"Sorry to bother you. Are you the masseuse?"

"Yes, I'm in the middle of a session right now. You'll have to wait until I'm done if you want a massage," he said as he was about to close the door.

Moro barked and the man stopped midway.

"I do not want a massage. I need to ask if you were in Leonardo Jones' RV this morning?"

Now realizing there was a crowd outside, he stood quietly for a minute before responding.

"What is this all about?"

"I need to know if you were in his trailer before starting on this client."

"Yes. I gave him a massage and then came here to Mr.

Wragg for his appointment. Again, I ask, what is this all about?"

"It seems there's been an accident and I'm just trying to establish a timeline," Nana said.

"What kind of an accident? When I left him, he was perfectly fine."

"He is dead."

She waited for his reaction.

"Wait just one minute! Are you accusing me of something? I didn't do anything. I went to give him a massage and that is all," Henry sounded nervous.

"I'm not accusing you of anything. The authorities have been called. Please make sure you do not leave the area," Nana told him in an authoritative voice.

"Of course. Let me finish up with Mr. Wragg and I'll be right out."

The masseuse closed the door and Nana turned around to address the crowd. She could tell that as the news spread, people had started speculating. Some were whispering, while others appeared horrified by the news that one of their own had been found dead.

Sally, had just wiped a tear off her cheek before turning to one of the campers who had approached her asking if she was alright. It was evident that she was distraught.

At that moment, Valdez pulled up in his golf cart with a police officer next to him, soon followed by two cruisers.

Nana approached Valdez. He knew from speaking with Eddie and Juana that she'd worked previous investigations. She'd even been instrumental in finding the culprit who had tried to kill her.

"Valdez."

"Nana."

He asked her asked what had happened.

"It appears Leonardo Jones is dead. His wife, Sally," she said as she pointed to the woman sitting in the chair, "found him and then came out of their RV screaming. It was loud enough that immediately a crowd formed."

"Alright, what else can you tell us?" the police officer standing next to Valdez asked.

"Oh, sorry. This is our local Sheriff, Alfredo Fisher. This is …"

"Rosalia Gomez, but most call me, Nana," she said before he could say anything further.

"Ms. Gomez, please go ahead, continue."

"Alright. Once Sally came out screaming, I approached her and asked her to tell me what had happened. At first, she was non-responsive. She just continued to scream. Eventually, I was able to calm her down enough to have her sit in the chair. When I asked her again what had happened, she pointed to her RV. At that point, I carefully opened the door, it was already ajar, with my foot and entered."

"And, what did you find?"

"Mr. Jones lying on the floor in a fetal position with a towel around his waist. No sign of a struggle. He did appear to have vomited and he had a runny nose."

The Sheriff turned towards one of the officers and instructed him to go inside. To the second officer, he instructed to secure the perimeter. The third officer walked over to Sally and started to ask her questions.

"Anything else you can tell me?" Sheriff Fisher asked.

"Actually, yes. I did confirm he had just had a massage. The masseuse is now in that RV," she said as she pointed, "he knows that Mr. Jones is dead because I told him after I confirmed he had received a massage. He assured me he would be right out as soon as he finished his session with Mr. Wragg."

Just then the door to the RV opened. The masseuse exited, closed the door, and walked up to the Sheriff.

"Sir, I'm Sheriff Fisher. I understand you gave Leonardo Jones a massage recently?"

"Yes, but I didn't kill him."

"I never said anything about killing him. What is your name and how did you end up coming on-site for the massage?" Sheriff asked as he took out his notebook.

"My name is Henry, Henry Finch. I was asked to come to the campground by Valdez who has invited me on occasion in the past to offer my services to the campers."

"Did you notice anything wrong with Mr. Jones during his massage? Or did he say anything to indicate he was in distress or concerned about someone wanting to harm him?"

"No. Nothing of the sort."

"Did you see anyone lurking around?"

"Lurking around? No. I did, however, have to step out to my car for a moment, if that helps."

"How long were you gone?"

"Just a few minutes. My car is parked over there by the main entrance to the campground. I was gone only as long as it takes to walk over there, and then walk back. But again, I didn't kill him. I had never even seen him before today," he sounded stressed.

Now he sounded stressed.

Nana looked directly at Henry and decided it was time she read his mind. *Curious*, she thought to herself as she read his thoughts. *He is lying about not knowing him. Now that is strange, why would he lie about something like that unless he was guilty?*

She decided to keep that information to herself for now. It wasn't as if she could tell the Sheriff she reads minds. Even if she wanted to, he'd think she was crazy. And, then he wouldn't allow her to work alongside him on the case.

"Alright, Mr. Finch. Give the deputy over there your information and we'll be in touch. You are free to go for now," he said as he pointed to one of the police officers standing by Sally.

At that point, Nana noticed Sally seemed to have

composed herself enough that she was smiling. As a matter of fact, Mario had walked up to Sally and was consoling her. This was her opportunity to find out more about him.

Turning to the Sheriff she asked if there was anything else he needed from her, otherwise she would check on Sally.

"Go ahead. Valdez has told me a little about you and I'm certain I'll be reaching out personally to speak with you soon. I understand you'll be here for a year. So, I ask that you do not leave the campground until further notice."

"I have no intention of leaving. Don't worry. I'll be around if you need me. Looking forward to working this case with you," Nana said with a smile as she waved and walked away.

Sheriff Fisher just stared at her without uttering a word. Taking a deep breath, he raised his eyebrows and walked in the direction of the RV.

It seemed to Nana as if the area had been invaded by police and the crowd had now grown substantially. Nana walked up to Sally and Mario.

"Just checking to see how you are holding up?"

Sally looked at Nana and responded.

"Thank you so very much for taking care of me. Everything is a blur right now, but I do know you brought me here to this chair and made sure I sat down before I fainted. So, for that, I want to thank you."

"No problem. I'm sorry for your loss," she said as she looked directly at the man standing next to Sally.

"Hello, again," Nana said as she extended her hand.

"Hello," he said as he looked at Nana.

"Didn't I see you awhile back on the weekend trip that Sally and Leonardo went on in the Keys?" Nana asked certain he flinched.

"Oh, yes. I didn't realize you had been on that trip," he replied as he looked at Sally.

Not wanting to make the situation any more awkward than it was, Nana told them both she was going to her caravan to change. She then placed her hand on Sally's shoulder and let her know if there was anything she needed to not hesitate to ask, and with that she walked to her caravan. Juana had been watching.

When she was certain no one was following her, she walked up to Nana's caravan and knocked.

"Just a moment," Nana called out.

She opened the door to see a distressed Juana standing there nodding her head.

"Come inside Juana."

Juana closed the door behind her and sat on the couch.

"Nana, I can't believe you went into the RV. You are so brave. I never would've done that," Juana whispered.

"Unfortunately, I've seen enough death it doesn't affect me like other people. It is very sad about Leonardo. I do wonder though who hated him enough to kill him?" Nana said mostly to herself.

"Killed?" "I thought he died of a heart attack? Are you certain it was murder? I can't think of anyone who would want him dead. It's crazy, this is a good, fun group. Yes, that time you went with us was a bit odd, but as I previously mentioned it is not normal."

"Juana, I told you already. It was not your fault, and as you can see, I went and purchased my own caravan. So, those incidents didn't deter me from joining your club. Now, can you think of anyone who would want him dead?"

"No, not really. I mean I know he and Sally were always fighting. But afterwards, when they made up, they were like newlyweds. Kissing and holding hands."

"There were a few signs on the body that led me to believe it may not have been from natural causes. So, do you happen to know anything about Henry Finch? Have you ever had a massage with him in the past?"

Juana thought about it and then remembered.

"I was scheduled for a massage last time we were all here,

but had to cancel. Can't remember the reason, but I never ended up having a session with him. From what I've heard though he was liked by everyone. As a matter of fact, I had scheduled one for Eddie and myself for next week," Juana responded.

"How about Roger? Do you know him?"

"No, I've never met him before. He might be one of those campers Valdez is now charging to use the grounds. You would have to ask him, sorry."

"How about Mario?"

"Mario is one of the club members. For the longest time he'd only travel with us sporadically. Lately, he's been going on all of our trips. This time I believe he's staying for a year like us."

"Thank you for answering my questions, and don't worry about anything. As I already mentioned, I plan on sticking around for a long time," Nana replied with a smile.

Juana was grateful that she had been so calm about the whole situation. Nana wondered ... she couldn't imagine anyone who would want someone like Leonardo dead. By all accounts, he appeared to be pleasant, friendly, and always available to lend a hand whenever anyone needed help.

Juana and Nana stayed together chatting some more. At one point, Juana asked if she could do a tarot card reading. She encouraged Nana to see if there was any possible way, she could find out something about the murder from the cards. Nana revealed she'd been thinking about it, and thanked her for the suggestion.

They decided to head back to the crime scene to see if there were any updates on the case. After what seemed like hours, the coroner concluded his preliminary investigation, the RV had been secured with yellow tape, and everyone had been instructed to stay away.

The Sheriff did, however, allow Sally to enter the RV accompanied by an officer to retrieve her personal belongings. She informed him she'd be staying in one of the guest rooms behind the main house. A row of rooms had been built for family and friends of the campers and she would be placed there until she could return to her RV.

After the police officers had left, only Sheriff Fisher, Valdez, Nana, Eddie and Juana remained.

"Let's head over to my office for coffee," Valdez said as he let Olga know they were returning soon," I'll see you shortly."

Valdez and Sheriff Fisher drove off in the golf cart. The rest walked to the main house, only a short distance away. Once everyone arrived, Olga was placing a freshly brewed pot of coffee and a plate of pastries on the round table inside Valdez' office. One by one, they entered the office and Eddie, the last one to enter, closed the door behind him.

Eddie, Juana, and Nana sat on the couch, Sheriff Fisher in one of the chairs, and Valdez behind his desk. He was the first to speak.

"I asked you all here to let Sheriff Fisher understand Nana's role in past cases. As I mentioned to him already, she's been instrumental in various investigations. This information was passed on to me by Eddie and Juana."

Nana looked at Eddie and smiled. She could tell Valdez knew about her tarot card readings, but remained silent.

"Sorry, Nana. It's just that I was so impressed with the stories Juana had previously told me, I wanted to share with Valdez that you might be able to help in this investigation. Besides, you've never been wrong with the cards, so when this all happened, I sent Valdez a text. I'm assuming he read it before he arrived with the Sheriff."

Valdez nodded in agreement.

"That explains a lot. No problem, Eddie. I would not have said a word if you had not mentioned it to Valdez," Nana said as she looked directly at the Sheriff.

"Sheriff, it's true. I have in the past worked closely with the Sheriff of Colten Island. That's where I live, and where I almost died over a year ago when someone I knew and trusted tried to kill me. That's the reason I'm here. I had decided I needed a vacation, so I bought a caravan and the rest is history."

Nana neglected to mention to anyone in the room that she could also read their minds. Moro stayed close to her and remained quiet during this interaction. At that point, she opened up her mind to see how she needed to proceed. Pleasantly surprised, she surmised that the Sheriff welcomed any help, as did Valdez. When she had closed her mind, Moro looked up at her.

Guess, we're getting involved?

"Yes, it seems we have a mystery on our hands and we need to figure out if indeed Leonardo was killed or if his death was a result of natural causes," she replied to Moro, but looked at the group making it appear she was addressing them directly.

"I can't believe this is happening. First a girl goes missing and now a dead man in an RV," Sheriff Fisher said under his breath.

"Wait, what? A girl is missing?" Valdez asked.

"Yes, that's where we were when we got the call about this victim. It appears a girl was camping with her friends yesterday. Not on your property, just on the border of your land on the north side. Sometime in the night she walked away and never returned. Her friends waited until this morning to call us because they thought maybe she had met someone and had stayed out all night."

Nana wondered if there was a connection. What were the odds of a disappearance and a murder happening so close together in a place that hadn't had any kind of problems in all the time that Valdez had started opening up the land to campers.

"Do you think there's a connection between the missing girl and Leonardo?" Nana asked.

"No. I don't see why there would be," he said trying to sound confident, although it came across as unsure.

Olga approached them to say that a camper wanted to speak with the Sheriff.

"Please bring him in," Valdez replied.

In walked a tall man with salt and pepper hair. He was dressed in jeans, loafers and a blue polo shirt.

"Thank you for seeing me, Sheriff. My name is Roger and I'm one of the campers here. I don't think it's anything, but I did see Henry walk out of the RV earlier this morning. He was gone for a while and then returned. It was bothering me enough I felt I needed to share this information with you. Again, I don't think he did anything, but I found it strange that he left without his table, and then returned within the span of half an hour," he said as he looked around the room.

"Did you see anyone enter or leave the RV while Henry was gone?" Sheriff Fisher asked.

"Well, I'm not certain."

"What do you mean you're not certain? Did you or did you not see someone around the RV? It's a simple question."

"I thought I saw someone leaving the area of the RV, but I'm not certain. It was more like a shadow. I was bending over to tie my shoelace and noticed what appeared to be feet running. When I looked again though, there was no one there. So, I'm not certain if it was my imagination or if I actually saw someone. And, if I did see someone, I can't tell you who it was, sorry."

"Thank you for coming forward. I'll follow up on this, and if I need to ask you anything further, I'll reach out. Make sure you don't leave the campground without speaking with me," Sheriff Fisher said.

Roger confirmed with everyone there he had no intention of leaving the campground anytime soon, and then exited the office. After what appeared to be minutes, Nana spoke.

"Sheriff, can you tell me about the missing girl?"

He looked at her a few seconds.

"Don't worry Sheriff, you don't have to worry about me. You'll see that I will turn out to be an asset. And if per chance you feel I've overstepped myself, I'll walk away without revealing to anyone the things I have learned, assuming there was anything at all to reveal," Nana said with a smile.

Sheriff Fisher knew he was in over his head, and knew he needed help.

"You can even reach out to Sheriff Storm who is in charge of Colten Island. He will vouch for me if necessary."

It couldn't hurt to have a fresh pair of eyes. So, he agreed to let her work alongside him, at least for now.

"So, what can you tell me about the missing girl?" she asked again.

"Well, it's not really a girl; Female, aged 42. Although I've been told Sasha, that's the victim, looks young for her age, Caucasian, medium built."

"Any sign of a struggle in the surrounding area where she was camping?"

"Now that you mention it, there were two sets of prints. However, they were far off in the distance and didn't seem to lead to their campsite."

"I see."

"Why do you ask? What is it you're thinking?"

Nana didn't want to accuse anyone without proof. Instead, she told Sheriff Fisher that she was only trying to establish a time-line to see what similarities there may be between the two cases, if any.

Sheriff Fisher didn't believe there was a connection. One case was about a missing person, the other a possible murder. He was starting to wonder if he should rethink allowing her to be part of the investigation.

"I can assure you Sheriff Fisher; I do not ask questions to ask them. I also don't jump to conclusions. You can trust that eventually I will help you find the killer or killers," she replied, not caring at that moment if he found it odd that she said what she said as if she could read his mind.

"As I mentioned, there are no similarities. At least for now, none that I could ascertain," Sheriff Fisher responded.

He was still on the fence about her abilities. For now, he'd watch her, and if she became a problem, he'd block her from having access to the investigation.

Sheriff Fisher's phone rang.

"Sheriff here," he answered.

Not being able to hear the caller clearly, Sheriff Fisher moved to the corner of the room. Everyone stopped talking and watched him. After he hung up he looked at the group and informed them the coroner had come to a conclusion about the cause of death.

"It appears he'll be able to give me a definitive answer once he's concluded the autopsy, however, by all indications, Leonardo was poisoned."

Everyone gasped at hearing the cause of death, except Nana.

"Poison? From getting a massage?" Valdez asked.

"Not necessarily from the massage itself. What he noticed was the way the body appeared - swollen, blotchy, and the fact that he'd vomited. They were able to get a sample to prove there was a large amount of peanut in his system. Before he made any further assumptions, he called Sally. She confirmed that Leonardo was allergic to peanuts. So, based on this new information, he's certain this could have been the cause of death. It appears there was a large amount in his body, enough to kill someone who is allergic," he said as he looked around the room.

No one spoke.

Sheriff Fisher knew he needed to question Sally more thoroughly now that he knew more about the cause of death. While he was discussing the coroner's findings, Nana thought she'd visit Sally later that evening and offer to do a tarot card reading. She'd tell her it might help find the killer.

After a few minutes, Sheriff Fisher excused himself, saying he needed to get back to the scene of the crime to see how his officers were doing. He mentioned to Nana that he'd give her a call soon, and then bid them farewell.

Once he was gone, Valdez told Eddie, Juana and Nana to make sure everything that was discussed in the room remained confidential. They were not to discuss anything they'd learned today with anyone in the club or any of the other campers.

Everyone promised to keep everything to themselves and when it was evident the meeting was over, they stood to leave.

"If you need anything, let me know. Otherwise, come out to this evening's entertainment show. It'll be a good opportunity to see everyone and how they behave. Hopefully by then we'll get word that the missing woman has been found," Valdez said as he stood and walked them to the door.

They thanked him for everything and agreed to see him later. Together they walked back to their caravans; Eddie and Juana, and, Nana and Moro. After a few minutes of silence, Juana spoke.

"Maybe we should have him," Juana pointed to Moro, "do our sniffing for us?" she said chuckling.

"You know Juana … that's not such a bad idea. I think I may just take him around to see if he can spot anything unusual."

Moro barked as if agreeing. Everyone responded by laughing.

When they got to their respective caravans, they bid each other a goodbye. Eddie and Juana were going to make some drinks and then sit outside. Nana said she'd take a nap.

Nana walked up to her door, and entered, closing it behind them.

As Nana walked in, she noticed Matilda. Ignoring her, she stretched, and as she was doing so, reminisced about the previous night. It had been quite a delightful evening filled with margaritas and lots of joyful chatting. One of the campers had brought out his guitar and entertained the group. Others had even joined in singing the lyrics to the music being played.

Needless to say, that was not what had happened that first weekend trip she took with Juana and Eddie. This time around however, it felt as if things were different, and that made her happy.

Last night, everyone who sat around the fire was engaging. Linda and her beau talked about how they met. Sally and the man sitting next to her laughed a lot and once in a while he'd whisper something to Sally where she feigned embarrassment. Even Bill appeared to be pleasant. Although he did disappear for a while during the night, returning at one point flustered.

"Matilda!" Nana called out.

The room became cold and Matilda reappeared.

"You summoned, oh master?" Matilda said laughing so hard parts of her were translucent.

"Very funny. I called you because as you are well aware by now, there's been a murder. And, I am finding that being here is something I'd like to continue to do. However, if this case is not solved soon, we will have no choice but to pick up and leave. Furthermore, if we do leave, I'm thinking I might just get rid of this here caravan as I won't have a need for it anymore."

Matilda stopped in midair and the room became even colder. Nana figured that would do the trick. A little drama to get her attention.

"You can't sell the caravan. You're the only one in … I don't even know how long … who can see me and talk to me. You're the only one who the crystal ball has reacted to."

Taking what amounted to a deep breath, Matilda looked directly at Nana and asked what she wanted.

"What I want Matilda is for you to stop nagging me about your crystal ball. I also want you to tell me how you came to be attached to this caravan."

"That's all? Fine," Matilda answered as she materialized.

"Wait, you seem real?" Nana asked, shocked that she looked like a regular person.

"Yes, although I don't do it often as it takes a lot of energy."

She was already starting to fade.

Before Nana could say anything else, she was gone.

I guess that was too much for her, but I'm sure she'll return, Nana thought to herself.

Instead of waiting for Matilda to materialize, Nana decided to check out the panel where the crystal ball was stored. Maybe it could help her find the culprit. Reading minds didn't always give the results she needed and this case needed to be solved as soon as possible or a major travesty could take place.

Nana approached the panel and taped it just as she had the last time. The door easily opened exposing the crystal ball. As she grabbed it, she could feel her fingers tingle. Picking it up carefully, she placed it on her table.

There was a knock on the door. Juana opened the door without waiting for a response. The moment she saw the crystal ball she was elated.

"Is that what I think it is? Wow," Juana said as she stared at the ball.

Nana not having a reason to lie, told her the truth.

"Yes, it actually came with the caravan. It belonged to the original owner."

"That is so cool. Does it work?"

Nana was not certain, although as she touched the crystal ball it felt warm in her hands. She felt the tingle again in her fingers. This time it crept up her arms the longer she held on.

"What's supposed to happen now?" Juana asked unsure of what she expected to see.

Before she could answer, a vision of a ring appeared. *A ring*, she thought to herself as she held on to the crystal ball.

"Are you seeing anything Nana?" Juana asked.

Nana glanced at Juana seeing her eyes twinkle, hopeful something would materialize. Instead of answering she nodded.

"Can't you try again? I think you did see something, tell me please, whatever it is I can take it."

Nana wasn't sure if she should say anything, but the tingling continued, and the crystal ball grew even warmer than before.

"Juana tranquila. Let me concentrate. Un momento," Nana said as watched the crystal ball begin to fog.

Looking at Juana she asked if she could see anything in the crystal ball.

"No. It's clear. Am I supposed to see something?" she asked confused.

"Está bien. No, I just need you to focus on what you want answered. Keep the question to yourself," Nana said as the vision of the same ring appeared again.

Now the crystal ball had completely fogged. Then as she focused, she saw Eddie holding a ring.

Here goes nothing, she thought to herself.

"Juana, I want you to know this is the first time I have ever used a crystal ball. I'm not even certain this will work."

"It doesn't matter. You must try. I know you can do it Nana, please," she said with an urgency in her voice.

"Alright," Nana said as she concentrated on the crystal ball.

She closed her eyes for a moment and then opened them back up.

"I see Eddie holding a ring."

"Dios mio, that's it! That's exactly what I was thinking about," Juana said as she clapped.

"It is?"

"Si, Eddie last night gave me the most beautiful emerald ring. He said it was because he loved me so much. He wants us to renew our vows."

"Felicidades Juana. I'm so happy for you. When are you planning on renewing your vows?"

"Well, I wasn't going to do it. I thought it was silly, but now that you are seeing him with the ring ..."

"I think you should plan on renewing your vows. It will be so exciting, and if you want, I'm more than happy to organize it for you?

"That would be wonderful, but nothing fancy. Just our club members. Wait until I tell Eddie."

"No!" Nana said in a loud voice startling Juana.

"But why? This is exciting news."

"No, Juana. You cannot tell anyone right now about the crystal ball. We have a killer on the loose and I don't want anyone thinking I can identify them before I've had a chance to confirm who that person might be."

"Oh, you think one of the camper's is a killer?"

"Yes."

Nana was starting to think Bill was the killer. His anger, behavior, and overall demeanor was something she couldn't stop thinking about. The thoughts that went through his head called him out as a person who didn't hold back if he became enraged. The possibility was there that he had an argument with Leonardo and killed him. That's the likely scenario, now all she had to do was prove it was him.

While Nana was thinking about Bill, Juana kept repeating over and over again in her mind that all she wanted was for things to go back to the way they'd been when they first joined the club.

Despite the fact that things were different, it wasn't all bad. There were new members who brought a sense of adventure to the club.

Nana could tell Juana was not happy at the moment. She needed to find a way to assure her that things would be fine. So, she brought the conversation back to the ring.

"Do you have any ideas on what you want or do I have open reign to organize it for you?"

"I hadn't thought about it. This was so unlike Eddie; I'm still trying to get used to the idea that he bought me a ring and asked me to renew our vows. I trust you completely Nana, so, anything you do will be spectacular," Juana said with a smile.

They briefly discussed ideas on where to have the event and other logistics, and Nana promised her again that she didn't need to worry about anything including the murder. Everything would be fine.

After Juana left, Matilda materialized.

Thank you for picking up and using my crystal ball. The humming has stopped and for that I'm grateful.

"Yeah, what's that all about anyway?"

I really don't know. I've stayed away for a long time because the humming was driving me crazy, besides the fact that no one has had the ability to see me or speak to me. There's only been a few owners, but I've scared them all away. They were useless. Not a single one of them found the crystal ball. And, before you ask me the reason the workers didn't find it, it was because every time they got close, I would distract them enough to forget about the panel. You see, the only thing I'm certain about is that the person who finds the crystal ball must be the owner of the caravan.

"Ya entiendo. Although, I'm curious as to why you're still here attached to the caravan?"

I never saw a light or anyone show up to tell me where I needed to go. So, I stayed, Matilda said rather somber.

Taking a deep breath Nana thought she'd regret her decision, but she was curious to find out the story behind Matilda. Besides, it seemed like she wasn't going anywhere, at least, not anytime soon.

"The crystal ball seems to be working. The strangest thing happened when I touched it. An image appeared and when I mentioned it to Juana, it was exactly what she'd been thinking about and visualizing."

That's the way it works. The crystal ball becomes foggy and warm to the touch, and then the visions appear. Visions that can only be seen by the seer. In this instance, that is you. This is how I'd do readings.

"Si," Nana said with a nod. "When I do my tarot card readings, that's exactly what happens."

Maybe you can use it to figure out who killed that camper. I'm starting to get used to having you around and I don't want you to get rid of the caravan. That would mean I'd be alone again.

Nana realized that although Matilda had been rather annoying since she first met her, it was obvious she was also very lonely. Maybe having her around wouldn't be the worst that could happen. A thought occurred to her that if Matilda was willing to try and figure out who killed Leonardo that she might be useful in spying on the Miami Coastal Caravan Club members until they could narrow down a list of suspects.

If Matilda was a lonely as Nana imagined, then this might just keep her busy and out of her hair.

❖

———

❖

Chapter 5

S everal weeks had passed since the body of Leonardo
had been found. Sally was still staying in one of the
rooms in the Main House. Even though she'd been
given the OK to move back into the RV, she had chosen to
delay the move.

To date, there were no new clues regarding Leonardo, and
Sheriff Fisher was starting to get frustrated with the case.
Even the camper was still missing and by now her friends
had packed up and left.

Everything had gone back to normal. Friends were hiking
together, hanging out in the evening, and a few new campers
from the club had joined last minute. Nana wondered if it
was time to start reading the club member's mind to get a
better idea of what they were thinking. Someone had to know
something or think of something useful.

Just as she was contemplating reaching out to Raul, Rosa's
spirit guide, there was knock on the door. Moro's ears perked
up and he let her know the visitor was Bill. For a split-second
Nana thought about ignoring him.

"Nana, it's Bill. Are you here?"

Taking a deep breath, she told him the door was unlocked.

Walking inside he looked around and told her she shouldn't leave the door unlocked.

"You have to be careful, a crazy person could come inside," he said as he tried to be funny.

She ignored his futile attempt at being humorous.

"Bill, to what do I owe this visit?"

"I thought I'd come to see how you are doing since I know you're the one who saw Leonardo's body. It must have been a shock," Bill said.

"Yes, it was a shock. The poor man. Do you know who could have wanted him dead?"

"No. I have no idea. Why are you asking me?" he replied in a defensive tone.

"I didn't mean anything by it, it's just since you've known him longer than me, I thought maybe you had some idea of who could have done this?"

Bill pulled back and uncrossed his arms. She had stuck a chord; of that she was certain.

"Well, I can see you're doing alright. I'm off to meet up with some friends. See you later," Bill said as he briefly stared at her before walking out of the caravan.

"Now, that was strange," Nana said to Moro.

He's strange.

"Por seguro! You hit the nail on the head."

———

S heriff Fisher felt exhausted. He was stuck and couldn't come up with a plausible reason why someone would want to kill Leonardo. From everything he had learned, he was a likable person. Friendly to everyone and always willing to lend a helping hand.

There was the inheritance, but no one except Sally benefited from his death and even though he'd heard they quarreled often there was no indication he was going to cut her out of the will, or was planning on leaving her.

As Sheriff Fisher leaned back in his chair, he sighed, and then closed his eyes. He wondered if there was a connection between Leonardo and the missing camper. Although he had told Nana there was not, he wondered if he had answered in haste.

He sat up and stared at the board. On the left side was the picture of Leonardo. Under that was a picture of his wife Sally, and under that he had written the words inheritance, and next to it millionaire. Then he wrote motive, and next to that a question mark.

Next in big letters he wrote "suspects." Obviously, nothing came to mind so he left it blank. He needed to question everyone at the campsite again. The first stop would be Nana as she seemed to be familiar with many of the club members.

On the right side of the board, he put the picture of the missing camper. Under her picture he had written her name Sasha Tripp. Single, no known boyfriend or lover. Age 42. Profession, barista. Last seen - the same day that Leonardo was found dead.

It didn't appear they had crossed paths. They didn't hang out in the same circles or even share the same friends. As far as he knew, they hadn't even seen each other at the campground. Valdez had done a pretty good job in separating the friends and family from the paying guests. Although anyone could wander into the other campsite without a problem.

"Well, this was going nowhere. I'm going to head back to the campsite," he yelled out to no one in particular. The officers nodded and returned to what they were doing.

Sheriff Fisher walked out of the station and got into his cruiser. Lost in thought he didn't notice someone standing outside his window looking at his board.

———

A ding sounded on her phone indicating a text. Nana looked at the message then at Moro.

"Juana and Eddie are going to a festival in the next town over. Want to join or would you prefer to stay here relaxing?"

I'm always up for going out.

Laughing she knew that'd be his answer. She just wanted to mess with him.

October in Vermont was spectacular. Some of the leaves had already turned red and yellow. The weather was crisp, but not so cold as to require a jacket. She called out to Matilda to let her know she was heading out and to keep an eye on things.

Just as she was gathering her purse there was a knock on her door. Assuming it was Juana she called out.

"I'm coming out now. Hold on."

When she opened the door, she was surprised to see instead Sheriff Fisher standing there with a smile on his face.

"It looks like I caught you on your way out?"

Nana didn't have to read his mind to see how exhausted and frustrated he seemed. She thought maybe she should stay behind and see what he needed.

"I was going to go to a festival in the next town, but I can go another time. I think it's best if I stay," she said as she pointed to the couch.

"Are you sure?"

"Absolutely. Let me just let Juana and Eddie know that I'll either meet up with them later or I can go another day."

Nana walked out of the caravan to speak with Eddie and Juana as Sheriff Fisher looked more closely at the inside of the caravan. He was impressed with the molding and the crafts-manship of the interior. The colors she had chosen to decorate were vibrant, yet welcoming.

Then he felt a sudden drop in temperature. He looked around perplexed. He couldn't for the life of him tell what had caused the sudden change. What he didn't know was that Matilda had appeared when she heard his voice. She was standing right next to him.

Just then Nana returned.

"Matilda, what are you doing?" she screamed out making Sheriff Fisher jump from the couch.

"Who's Matilda? Where is this, Matilda?" he asked as he looked around the caravan.

He couldn't see anyone there except Nana and Moro.

Nana closed her eyes before responding.

"Sorry, I, well …"

"Are you having a seizure or something?"

Now she had to laugh.

"Sit down please," she said as she pointed to the couch.

He did as he was told because his initial assessment was this woman was not crazy. So, he was intrigued to see what she had to say about all this babbling.

"I want you to keep an open mind. I'm not sure how much you actually know about me, but sometimes I can sense when a ghost is around. When I purchased this vintage caravan, I started to feel cold air over and over again randomly in different spots. As I researched, I found out that it was believed to be haunted by the original owner, Matilda."

She waited for him to say something, and when he didn't, she continued. Even though she was completely fibbing she hoped it was just enough to make him believe she wasn't crazy.

"Anyway, I have called out to it when I have felt the temperature drop and when I've asked it to go away the temperature has returned to normal. So, I'm assuming I'm talking to Matilda. When I came inside, I felt it was so cold the only explanation was that Matilda was here."

"You talk to ghosts?"

"Oh, no that would be crazy," she chuckled.

"But you just said…"

"No, I don't actually have a conversation with them," she replied eyeing Matilda who seemed to be enjoying seeing Nana stumble for the right words and seeing Sheriff Fisher debating whether or not to run and never look back or hear her out.

"I just figured if she is really here, I wanted to know what she was doing even though I didn't expect her to answer me," again she said this as she looked directly at Matilda who just shrugged.

"Alright, for a minute there I thought you were going to turn out to be one of those wackos that says they can talk to the dead."

"That would be silly. Anyway, I'm assuming you came by to ask me something?" she asked as she shushed Matilda away with her arm behind her back.

No way am I leaving, I'm having too much fun.

Acting as if nothing was out of the ordinary, Nana started to make some Cuban coffee.

"I'm making some coffee if you'd like some?"

"Sure, that sounds like a good idea. Thank you."

She turned her back to him and tried to count. Mentally, she sent Moro a plea for help with Matilda. He ignored her as he too wondered what was going to happen next.

Great, she thought to herself. They are now in cahoots with each other. Por Dios.

"As soon as the coffee is ready why don't we go outside. It'll be warmer there," she said with a smile.

"Of course, take your time."

So, for the next few minutes they chatted about her and Colten Island. She told him about La Misteriosa Café. He asked about her brush with death. Nana told him she almost died, but thanks to some savvy people they were able to find the culprit and all was good in the end.

When the coffee was done, she turned around and told him to hold open the door. During all this time Matilda stood next to him just watching him. She had never seen anyone so attractive. Six feet, deep brown eyes, a five-o-clock shadow, and wavy dark black hair. She was enamored.

Once outside although it still felt cold, although at least Sheriff Fisher was not trembling. This time Matilda stood across from him to get a better view, making it possible for him to warm up. They stayed there for some time chatting.

"So, as I said earlier. I'm certain you came over to ask me something?"

"Yes, I was wondering if you could give me a breakdown of the club members?"

"Well, I don't personally know any of the club members except for Juana and Eddie. They are friends and Juana is also a client," she said expecting the next question.

"A client?"

"Yes, my clients come to me to have their tarot cards read."

Nana watched for his reaction hoping he wasn't a skeptic.

Sheriff Fisher wasn't sure if to believe in tarot cards as his experience in the past had not turned out well. The two people he had gone to see turned out to be fake. He had however, heard stories where people were told something that came true. So, he decided to keep an open mind, at least for now.

Before they continued talking if Nana was going to give him her impressions about what she thought was going on at the campground she thought it best to do so back inside the caravan.

"I'm sure the caravan's temperature is back to normal. Why don't we go back inside away from prying ears?" She got up and gathered the coffee cups.

"That's a wise idea."

All along, she was wondering if she should be honest and

tell him about the tarot cards or fib about this too and make some outlandish explanation that she hoped he'd buy. In the end, she decided to be honest with him.

Once inside Sheriff Fisher sat in the couch and Nana sat in the chair across from him. Matilda had finally gotten bored and had disappeared. Hopefully, she won't return until after Sheriff Fisher has departed.

"So, besides owning La Misteriosa Café I read tarot cards."

"Do you mind explaining to me how does this tarot thing work?"

He figured if she was the real deal, she could tell him how someone could look at a card and get an impression.

"Well, I can show you if you'd like?"

"You mean right now? No, that's alright. Just explain how it works if you don't mind."

It was obvious he was nervous and unsure that tarot card readings were legitimate. She'd have to tread carefully with him.

"No problem. So, there's a deck of cards. The client divides them into three stacks after I have shuffled them. I then put them all back into one pile and pull out the top three cards in the pile. These indicate the past, present, and future. That's all there is to it," she said as she looked for his reaction.

"How often are you wrong?"

Wow, she wasn't expecting that question from him. She thought he'd make a sly remark or something, but this… interesting.

"Well, according to my clients I'm never wrong," she replied with a smile.

In his mind he was mulling over the fact he had confirmed what he needed to know from Sheriff Storm of Colten Island. So, he was willing to even consider tarot card readings. Anything, if it would help with the investigation.

"Well, at this point I'm open to anything you have as I

have come to a roadblock on both cases," he responded sounding deflated.

"Let's see. I can tell you what I've observed since I've been here. Now, mind you some of it is just speculation and I have no proof whatsoever about any of it. I'll explain as I go along," she replied.

"Good. That'll work," he said as he took out his notebook and pencil.

"Leonardo. I have not known him for very long. On those times I saw him he was always friendly and smiling. He enjoyed spending time with the club members. I heard he had retired. Someone mentioned they had a modest RV until one day he showed up with the one he has now with no explanation except that he had won the lotto. I think there may be more to that, but I didn't have a chance to find out more."

"How about his wife?"

"Sally, is an interesting character. Every time I've seen her, she has complained about being here, and then several hours later she acts as if nothing had happened and is participating and laughing alongside everyone else. Leonardo was asked once why she came, and his response was that he always gave her the option to stay home, and every time she refused."

At this point Nana wondered if she should tell him about her suspicion concerning Sally and Mario?

"Anything else you can tell me about Sally?"

"Well, this is the part that is speculation. I've seen her before with Mario and the way they behave with each other seems overly friendly. I'm not saying there is anything going on there, but every time he's around she seems happy and laughing more than any other time."

———

"**W**hat do you mean Sheriff Fisher is at Nana's?"

"Exactly what I said. I saw him first sitting outside with her drinking Cafecitos. Then they went inside. I'm concerned he's over there discussing what happened. That snoopy Nana is going to ruin everything. I've been watching her ask questions thinking no one noticed her subtle inquiries. I know, I know exactly what she's doing and I'm getting worried. We need to do something before it's too late."

"Relax. There's no need to panic."

———

Back at the caravan Sheriff Fisher and Nana were talking.

"Are you saying that Sally and Mario are having an affair?" Sheriff Fisher was now interested.

"No. I don't have any proof of that. However, the first time I joined Juana and Eddie on one of these trips, I noticed something between Sally and Mario. When I was getting my breakfast one morning, I saw an RV enter the campground stop, and Sally climbed inside. She stayed there for a few minutes and then walked out. She never mentioned she knew the driver and I found out later it was Mario. However, when Leonardo was around, they were never together. It's really the little things, but those sometimes are enough to paint a picture."

"If Sally is having an affair with Mario that's motive," he said while he scribbled in his notebook.

"Can you tell me anything else about them?"

"No. Like I said it's more of a feeling, but I have no basis really for my assumption."

Nana knew this would get Sheriff Fisher looking into the

possible relationship and no one would think it was her suggestion.

"Can you tell me anything about Mario," he looked in his notebook for the last name, "Wragg."

"Him I know nothing about. He arrived at the campground shortly after us. Since Sally is staying in one of the rooms in the Main House, we don't see much of her and or him."

"I'm waiting for background checks on those two. We'll see what I find when I get the report. What about Linda McLean?"

"Linda is a very interesting sort," Nana responded wondering how to tell him what she saw when she read her mind without telling him she could read minds.

"Oh? What can you tell me about her?"

"I met her the first time I went camping and she was distraught because her boyfriend had left her. I read her the tarot cards and told her she'd meet someone. That seemed to make her happy. The next time I saw her was when we got here."

"Is the guy with her now the one you saw in your cards?"

"No."

"Would you like to elaborate?"

He asked curious to hear what she had to say.

"Not really. Nothing there really except that she seems happy now."

"Alright, moving on …tell me about Henry."

The masseuse, now he was interesting.

"Well, the day we found Leonardo's body was the first time I had seen him. I learned that he usually arrived a few days after the campers did. Then he returned sporadically throughout the time that there were campers. What I did notice was that he seemed nervous. I'm not certain if it was because he felt foolish about having left his client unattended or if there was something more to his behavior."

"I'll check to see if there have been any previous reports on him. That is very helpful. At least now I'm starting to get a better picture of everyone. When I tried to interview the club members no one gave me a straight answer. It's been difficult building a case when there are no clues and no cooperating witnesses."

"Don't worry, the truth always prevails. The true killer will be revealed soon."

Before he could ask her about Bill, his phone rang. After a brief conversation he hung up.

"I'm sorry Nana, but I must return to the station. There's been a new development and I can't delay."

"What happened?" Nana asked worried it might be another body.

"Honestly, I don't know. My Deputy called and said I was needed urgently back at the station and then hung up before I could ask what happened. We'll be in touch soon. Thank you again for answering my questions."

Sheriff Fisher stood and walked out of the caravan. He had not been gone more than a few seconds when Linda walked in.

"Nana are you alright?" she appeared concerned.

"Yes, why do you ask?"

"Because Sheriff Fisher was here for a while and then I saw him walk out of here abruptly," she replied.

Nana tried to read her mind, but there was so much rambling it was hard to figure out what she was actually thinking.

"He was questioning me again about what I saw on the day that we found Leonardo's body. Then he got a call and said he had to leave," Nana answered hoping she could read Linda's mind.

Before she could even try, Linda's demeanor changed drastically. Now, she was bubbly telling Nana about the guy staying with her. She thanked Nana again for the tarot card reading, and wanted her to know how happy she this session had made her. Even her mind said the same thing. Linda kept repeating over and over again how happy she was.

Nana wondered if she was trying to convince herself because no one repeats how happy they are, over and over, and over again. When she was finally able to get rid of Linda, she locked her door. This time she told Moro to not let anyone enter. She then turned around and called out to Matilda.

Where's the fire?

"Matilda, I need your help," Nana said as she paced the caravan.

My help? Of course. What do you need me to do?

"I need you to check out the club members and tell me if any of them are acting strange. If we don't figure out who killed Leonardo soon, I'm afraid there may be another death. We also have to look into the missing camper."

I can go and check on the club members. This is going to be fun. She twirled around the caravan, and then disappeared.

Nana couldn't help, but laugh at her. The longer she spent with Matilda the easier it was to accept she wasn't going anywhere and was now part of her life.

"Moro, I guess I'm not going to the festival today. Let's see if the crystal ball is any help."

She went to the secret panel and once the door opened, she carefully grabbed the crystal ball and transported it to her dining room table. There she removed the silk cover and rubbed it several times. Meanwhile Nana wondered about the killer.

The crystal ball began to get foggy, her fingers tingled and then the images came to her. First it was Leonardo sitting in his RV drinking a Cafécito. Then Sally climbing into their bed. Next it was Eddie and Juana taking a walk on the trail. She also saw Linda, Henry, Olga, and even Bill.

Now, she was more confused than before. Were they all involved in the murder? She would never believe Eddie and

Juana were responsible for the murder. Impossible. There had to be another explanation.

She rubbed the crystal ball again hoping the images would tell a better story. Nope. The scenes were different, but it was the same people again. What did it all mean? Nana was confused, and realized it was fruitless. Based on the few times she'd used the crystal ball she figured the story would come when it needed to come.

Nana put the crystal ball away, and closed the panel. She'd go back to it later. Taking a deep breath, she decided to go for a walk. It was early enough that she didn't have to worry about getting stuck out there in the dark.

"Moro, let's go for a walk. I don't want to go alone, but I need to think," she said as she grabbed his leash.

A leash?

"No, that's only in case anyone is on the trail and gets nervous when they see you."

Oh, alright. Let's go.

Moro barked several times, happy that he was going to explore more of the trail. Nana grabbed her keys, walked out and locked the door. She looked around, but didn't see anyone. *They must have all gone to the festival,* she thought to herself.

When they arrived at the start of the trail, she told Moro to stay close. But he was so excited he took off down the trail barking.

Nana thought about Leonardo and decided she needed to speak with everyone from the club, and the sooner the better. Someone had to know something. She was so focused on the crime; she didn't hear anyone come up behind her.

Then she felt the darkness surround her, and down she fell. Someone had come up behind her and hit her on the head. She wasn't dead, but had been dragged deeper into the woods away from the trail. Moro came back to the trail, where he thought Nana was, only to find she wasn't there.

He barked and called out to her.

Nana. Nana where are you?

Now he was worried. She normally would have answered immediately, and the fact that she wasn't responding was concerning.

Head down, he sniffed the area until he found her scent, and followed it. There, behind a tree, lay Nana. He nudged her and listened closely. Once he'd confirmed she was still alive he ran as fast as possible back to the campsite. The first persons he saw was Valdez. He stopped in front of him, barking and moving towards the woods in hopes the man would follow him.

Valdez was startled and thought the dog was going to bite him. He stood without moving. Moro realized his error, so he stood farther away barked once and then turned around towards the woods. He moved slightly towards the trail, and barked again.

"Do you want me to follow you?" Valdez thought he looked silly asking a dog a question.

However, Moro understood and barked twice, stood for a moment, then barked once more before he turned toward the trail again. This time, Valdez got the hint and started to follow him. Before long, they arrived where Nana was and this time, Moro continued to bark without stopping.

Immediately, Valdez checked her pulse and was happy to see she was alive. He took out his phone and called 911 explaining to the operator where they were on the trail. Luckily, they had just installed mile markers, and he was able to be exact. He called Olga and told her to find Eddie and Juana and that they would want to know she was probably going to the hospital.

Valdez remained close by until the paramedics arrived. Shortly after that, Sheriff Fisher appeared on the scene.

"What happened?"

"I'm not sure. I was close to the entrance to the trail when

Moro came running up to me barking. At first, I thought he was going to bite me, but then I realized he was trying to get my attention. I followed him into the woods and I found her here unconscious."

"Thank God she's alive," he said as the paramedics were placing her into the ambulance.

"I looked around, but I didn't see anyone near the area. I'm sorry I can't be of any further assistance," Valdez said with a frown.

"You found her, and that's huge," Sheriff Fisher replied, as he placed his hand on his shoulder.

"Thank you, my friend."

Valdez called Moro to follow him to the campsite. He hoped her caravan was opened so that he could place the dog inside, but they found it was locked. Moro barked. Valdez could tell he was upset. Finding a leash on the picnic table he approached Moro.

"Moro, I'm going to put the leash on you so that I can secure you out here. I don't want you getting lost and then have to explain to Nana that we lost you. I want to go back to the trail and see if there are any clues."

Valdez picked up the leash and as he walked over to Moro. He sat waiting for him to attach the leash to his collar. Once that was done, Valdez secured the leash to the leg of the table. He walked to the caravan next door and asked for a bowl to put down some water for him. Feeling comfortable he could leave the dog alone for a little while, he headed back to the spot where he had found Nana.

Sheriff Fisher and several officers were scouting the area.

"Fisher, find anything useful?"

"No. We're expanding the perimeter. Head back to the campsite and wait for me. I'll be there as soon as we're done here. Before you go, how is Nana?"

"Haven't heard anything. I do have her dog, Moro,

attached to the outside of her caravan. I'll go back now and check on him."

"Sounds good. Thanks. Talk soon," Sheriff Fisher replied.

He walked back to where one of his officers was bent over looking at some debris.

———

Nana, after being examined, had been taken to a private room. The doctor wanted to keep her overnight for observation.

"Mrs. Gomez, I'm Doctor Lawrence," he said as he read her chart.

"Call me Nana."

"Nana, you seem to have been hit over the head with a blunt object. We don't believe you have a concussion, but to rule it out I have ordered an MRI. Once I receive the results, I can make a better determination of whether to keep you or let you go."

"Thank you," Nana replied as she closed her eyes.

She had an excruciating headache.

"I can see you are in some kind of discomfort. Would you like something for your headache?"

"Yes, please."

"I'll send the nurse now with your medication, and return once I have reviewed the results of your MRI. Try to rest, you are in good hands."

Nana didn't have a chance to rest. Shortly after the doctor left, Eddie and Juana arrived, followed by the several other club members. One-by-one they stopped by to make sure she was alright. She had such a terrible headache she couldn't figure out who was thinking they hadn't hit her hard enough.

Did I imagine someone saying they should have hit me harder? Or is my imagination running wild, she thought to herself as she drifted into a deep sleep. By the time, she woke up for her

MRI test, everyone had gone leaving her alone with her thoughts.

She tried, she truly tried, but for the life of her she couldn't figure out who hit her. She must be getting close to the truth.

———

Nana had been home now for a few days. Still no news on who could have attacked her. So, she had decided to stay close to the caravan, with Moro and Matilda.

Juana came by frequently as did several of the club members. After being cooped up for almost a week she was ready to get back out in the world.

She called Juana and asked her if there was anything going on at the campsite, she was ready. Juana informed her they were having a themed party at the Main House. Everyone was to dress up in vintage attire, especially if you owned a caravan. Nana agreed that was the perfect distraction. So, they made a plan to go shopping the next morning in search of a costume.

Early the next day Nana rose feeling back to normal. She made Cafécito and toast, and shortly after that Juana called her to let her know she was ready to head out.

"Moro, you and Matilda take care of the place. If you see any suspicious characters scare them off."

You got it.

You can count on us.

"Gracias. See you guys later," Nana replied as she grabbed her purse and headed out.

The girls spent the morning going from second-hand store to vintage store, to even a Salvation Army store looking for just the right items to put together a stellar vintage outfit.

By lunch time, they were wiped out. They agreed that they

had everything they needed, and decided to go to lunch. It felt good to get out again and Nana was finally starting to feel like herself.

Juana told her all the gossip about the campground. How Sally was now seen spending time with Mario. Linda was still with her beau although they spent a lot of time fighting. Then there was Pedro and Miriam. She didn't know what was going on with them, but the fights were getting worse. He kept accusing her of cheating on him. She in return, accused him of killing the missing camper.

"Do you think he's capable of killing that woman?" Nana asked.

"I don't know. All I do know for certain is that most of the time they are fighting, and the few times they seem to be fine, one of them says something and then it starts all over again. No one really wants them around, but no one has said anything."

"How about Sheriff Fisher? Has he come around lately?" Nana was curious where he was with the investigations including her attack.

"He did come by a couple of times. He stopped only to speak with Valdez and Linda. Then he left without talking to anyone else."

"Curious. Wonder what that was all about?"

"Not certain, but it's time you took out your crystal ball and your tarot cards," Juana suggested.

"You know maybe if I "play" a gypsy during our party I can actually get a reading on these people. Although I'm afraid it would be deceitful to do a reading without telling them."

"Then you tell them you are doing a reading which you do. Just don't tell them you know they are the killer or attacker if that comes up. You might find yourself this time not just knocked out, but dead," Juana said.

"That's a great idea Juana. Gracias!"

B y the time Friday rolled around, Nana was ready for the party. She enjoyed dressing up in vintage clothing. Even Matilda approved of the outfit.

Nana had found a bright orange shawl with intricate embroidery that fit the look perfectly. She wore two skirts, one shorter than the other. The longest skirt was a rich purple, the shorter skirt had a pattern of different colors. The last item she had purchased was the headscarf. She found one with varying patterns that matched perfectly with the skirts and accented the white ruffled top.

Getting dressed inside the caravan turned out to be quite a challenge. The small bathroom mirror was angled in a way that it was difficult to see the whole outfit. She made a mental note to buy one of those long mirrors you can attach to the back of a door.

She had decided, at last minute, to purchase a wig. The brownish loose curls hung on her shoulders, and once she put on the headscarf, she was amazed at how much she looked the part.

Once she was fully dressed, she went to retrieve the crystal ball. She placed it on the dining room table. She also grabbed the black tablecloth she had purchased earlier which she thought would be perfect for the look.

She placed the crystal ball, its silk cover, her tarot cards, the tablecloth, incense and her incense stand inside a large bag. Olga had promised her she'd have a small table set up in the corner where she could see clients.

You look just like a gypsy, Matilda said amazed at Nana's transformation.

"Gracias Matilda. I do feel a bit different," Nana chuckled.

I'll be right there beside you, in case you need help.

Nana didn't think Matilda could offer any assistance, but she didn't want to be rude, so she just nodded her thanks.

"Alright, Moro, and of course Matilda, let's get this party started," Nana said as she headed to the door.

She was starting to feel like a child playing dress-up. Smiling she closed the door behind her, and just as she was about to step down the ladder, she tripped over the hem of one of her skirts.

Nana saw herself plunge headlong towards the ground when suddenly strong hands seized her and swung her out of harm's way, safely onto her feet.

"Nana, are you alright?"

She blinked and caught her breath before answering.

"Por Dios, how clumsy of me. Gracias for coming to my rescue," she replied, rather shaken.

"I'd heard you were going to be offering readings at the party, and came by to see if you needed help with anything. Lucky I was here."

"Thank you again, Bill. It was gallant of you to come to my rescue."

She dreaded trying to read his mind, but his change in demeanor was reason enough for her to try figure out what his plan was.

Just as she thought, he was curious if she really had the gift. If so, that worried him.

What could he possibly be hiding that he needed to know if she was the real deal? *Could he be Leonardo's killer,* she thought to herself. She sent Moro a message to make sure he kept an eye out and stayed closed. She didn't trust Bill.

"Can I escort you to the party?"

"I just have this bag to take, but we can walk together," Nana replied with a smile.

He took the bag from her. Nodding, she grabbed the side of her skirt to make sure she didn't have another incident. They walked together to the Main House.

Nana asked Bill how he had been doing. His responses

were rather vague. She did learn that he enjoyed his walks through the trails, and was having the best time of his life.

Odd, she thought to herself. *A very odd man.*

Before long they arrived at the Main House. It was already full of campers. There were even a few new faces Nana didn't recognize.

Olga noticed her immediately and walked up to them.

"Welcome. So glad you are both here. Nana, if you'll follow me, I can set you up where you'll be conducting your readings," she said as she pointed to the corner of the room.

Turning to Bill, Nana thanked him again, and took back her bag. She followed Olga relieved that he didn't follow them.

"Here's where I thought would be a good place for you to set up your things. Everyone can see you, and that should be incentive enough to come have a reading. If there's anything else you need, please just let me know."

"Gracias Olga. This is perfect," Nana replied with a smile.

Olga left, and Nana got to work. Within a few minutes she had set up her table, and was ready to greet her clients. They had decided that Olga would make the announcement that Nana was open for business later in the evening. Anyone that was interested in a reading was to fill out the sign-up sheet.

Nana decided before the announcement to mingle. She walked around the room chatting with everyone. Moro stayed by the table, but kept his eye on her. At one point, she could feel someone watching her, but when she looked around the room, she couldn't tell who it was.

By the time Olga was ready for her announcements the room was packed. Even Sheriff Fisher and several of his officers had stopped by for the party.

"Attention everyone. I just have a brief announcement. Valdez has asked me to mention a few things. First and foremost, thank you all for coming to our themed vintage party. It's great to see so many of you get into the spirit of dressing up. Most of you know Nana by now. She has offered to help make this evening even more authentic by doing readings. She has a crystal ball and tarot cards. Anyone interested in having a reading is to fill out the form on the table," she said as she pointed to Nana's table.

You could hear the responses from several of the members and they seemed pleased with this added feature. Olga continued.

"We want to make sure you have fun tonight. At the end of the evening, we'll announce the winner of the most realistic outfit. May the best man or woman win. Now, go have fun," she said as she put the microphone down.

The chatting continued until the food was brought out, then everyone headed for the buffet table. The rest of the evening, people mingled, ate, and danced.

When Nana thought it was time to start, she excused herself and headed to her table expecting to only see a few names. When she looked at the list, it appeared as if everyone in the room wanted a reading.

"Por Dios Moro, so many people want a reading. I hope I don't disappoint."

Nunca Nana. You're a pro. Now, let's get to work to see if we can find a killer.

Nana closed her eyes, said a silent prayer, and got ready to see her first client. By the time, Linda approached Nana had prepared everything.

"Welcome to Nana's Mystery Corner," she said with a smile.

Nana decided she'd get into character and have some fun.

"I love it," Linda clapped her hands.

She figured Linda would love the crystal ball, so she made an elaborate gesture as she removed the silk cover. Nana then closed her eyes and rubbed it.

The more she rubbed the crystal ball the foggier it got. Images began to appear. At first, Nana was confused because it didn't make any sense to her. So, she decided to just tell what she saw.

"What do you see? It looks clear to me. Do you see anything?" Linda was becoming impatient.

"I see a man, a man I recognize from the campground."

Linda's eyes grew wide and she covered her mouth with her hands showing her surprise.

"Is this someone you are interested in?"

"Yes, very much so."

Nana wondered about the guy she'd seen Linda with.

"Well, I see an interest there on both your parts. Seems like possibly a budding new relationship is in the air. I must caution you though, be careful where you tread."

Linda didn't listen to the last part. All she heard was the possibility of a new relationship. She'd been having fights lately and could tell her boyfriend was ready to hit the road. There was no way she'd be alone, so hearing this was just what she needed.

"Oh, thank you Nana. This is the best news I could've received. It's perfect," she said as she stood and walked away.

Again, Nana could feel someone watching her, but as she looked around the room, she still couldn't pinpoint who it was, and it was starting to rattle her.

The next appointment was Sheriff Fisher. Although he didn't really believe in any of this stuff, he'd heard so much about Nana he figured he'd check it out.

"Welcome to Nana's Mystery Corner," she said with a smile.

"I see how it is, you are definitely in character. I quite like it," he chuckled.

"So, young man. Close your eyes for a minute and think about what you want to know."

Nana started to rub the crystal ball and then opened her eyes.

She jumped up so abruptly she knocked over her chair.

"Dios Mio," she screamed as she covered her mouth.

Startled Sheriff Fisher also stood.

"What happened? What did you see?" he asked, alarmed.

"I … I … saw myself being killed."

❖

———

❖

Chapter 6

A few hours later Nana was still feeling rattled even though she assured Sheriff Fisher she was fine. She had tried to play it off as a joke, but Sheriff Fisher knew how to read people well enough to tell when someone was faking it, and Nana was not. She was actually frightened.

He had convinced her to take a walk with him, Moro in tow. They remained silent. Then when she had finally spoken, she told him she was sorry for her reaction. She'd never seen her own death.

After she had finished speaking, he asked.

"How certain are you it's your death. Maybe it's another attack, and now that you have foreseen it, maybe we can prevent it from happening."

"You know, you might be correct. I've always known the day when I'm going to die and what I saw isn't the way or time I'm going to die. I still have a few years left in me," she tried to sound humorous.

"Then we just need to figure out when this is supposed to happen, and prevent the person from hurting you. I'm going to assign a few patrolmen to watch over the campground just in case."

"That might actually be very helpful. Moro can do just so much," she replied with a strained smile.

"Of course, besides Moro is *just* a dog."

"Yeah, right. Just a dog," this time she chuckled.

The rest of the night had been strained. She didn't want to be there any longer, but she didn't want to disappoint the club members either.

Sheriff Fisher stayed closed by for the rest of the night. When she finished her last reading, she stood, indicating she had finished.

"How did it go? Did you see anything else that can help us identify who is going to attack you?" Sheriff Fisher was hopeful.

"No. Perdón, pero no."

"That's alright. I really didn't expect you to be able identify him or her that easily. We'll keep an eye on you and the camp. Something will turn up, don't worry. We'll catch the assailant."

He sounded confident.

Nana was grateful for his concern. The party the previous night had been in full swing when she finished, and because it looked like everyone was having such a great time, she had decided to stay only for a little bit longer and then excused herself.

Juana told her to go home and rest. She'd be by the next morning to see how she was feeling. Sheriff Fisher stated he was going to accompany Nana home.

Nana gathered all her belongings and then with Moro and Sheriff Fisher, left the party. They walked back in silence. When they arrived at the caravan, he told Nana to wait outside until he inspected the inside. She gave him her keys and he opened it up.

He walked around checking to make sure there was no

indication of a break-in, and that everything was where it was supposed to be. Satisfied, he exited the caravan and returned the keys to Nana.

"Looks good. You're safe to go inside. I'll wait here until I hear you lock your door, and then I'll head out. So, you know, one of the officers will be walking up and down the area. There will be someone close by at all times," Sheriff Fisher said.

"Gracias. I'm grateful for your concern. However, the more I think about it, I realize that I was concerned with finding the killer and a connection between Leonardo and the missing camper. I probably just let my mind play a trick on me."

Neither believed what she was saying.

"Well, goodnight, Nana."

"Hasta luego, Sheriff Fisher."

Nana locked the door and plopped into a chair. She covered her face for a moment when Matilda appeared. The shift in air was obvious to Nana.

Nana, I'm concerned about you. Who did you see?

"That's the problem, I couldn't see who it was. The person was blurry. All I did see, was being stabbed," she replied.

Well, after your abrupt behavior I stuck around for a bit to look at everyone to see if I saw any reaction. Mario smiled when you stood up and screamed. I found that odd. Then there was Linda. I'm not sure if she was happy or something else?

"I guess we need to look at Mario and Linda. I hope if it is them, that they are not working together. Eso sería el colmo. That would definitely be the worst."

As the day progressed, Nana kept herself busy with an array of chores. There was something wonderful about waking up to a group of friendly people, and she was not going to let anyone mess it up for her.

She decided to sit outside and do a crossword puzzle. It didn't take long before she was interrupted.

"Excuse me, I'm sorry to interrupt. I've heard talk around the campgrounds that you tell fortunes? Is that true?"

It was obvious that the woman wanted the answer to be yes. Something about the way she looked made Nana pay attention.

"Yes, is there something troubling you?"

The woman started crying.

Nana stood and guided her to the chair next to where she'd been sitting.

"Take your time and tell me what is troubling you," Nana spoke calming.

Just then one of the officers started to approach them. Nana gestured that everything was alright. He stood there for a few seconds, then proceeded to continue on his rounds.

Eventually, the woman stopped crying long enough to tell Nana the reason for her visit.

"I'm the mother of the missing camper. I was hoping you could do a reading and help me find my daughter."

This tugged at Nana's heart. She couldn't imagine what this woman must be going through, but the fact that she had stopped by was wonderful. Now, Nana could try to do a proper reading to see if she could help.

"Yes, the stories are true. Would you like me to do a reading for you?" Nana said

Nana already knew what her answer would be ahead of time.

"Oh, my. Yes, please that would be wonderful. I'm desperate to find my daughter."

"Give me a second while I go get my cards."

Nana returned with her cards and a glass of water for the woman.

"Let's start off with introductions. My name is Rosalia Gomez, but most call me Nana. And, you are?"

"I'm Alberta, and Sasha is my missing daughter."

"Let's get started. I need you to take this deck of cards,

and divide it into three parts. After you are done, I'll pick them up and divide them once more. Then you'll separate them one final time."

Nana was being extra careful to shuffle the cards enough to get a good reading. When Alberta was finished, Nana picked up the pile and shuffled them one last time. She then took out the first card, the second, and by the time the third card had been pulled out, she was convinced that Sasha had been murdered.

How to tell someone their child, regardless of their age, is no longer alive? It's just something that's not done, at least not in Nana's book.

"I'm sorry, it's a bit foggy. I see woods. There's an abandoned cottage, she might be there?"

Nana looked up and could see the hope building up. She felt terrible, but she wouldn't be the one to crash this women's hopes.

"I'm sorry I couldn't give you anymore. That happens sometimes," Nana said and placed a hand over Alberta's.

"Oh, dear. You've been wonderful. That's the most I have gotten since she disappeared. Right now, I'm grasping at straws. So, this is something. At this point, I resigned myself to thinking she is no longer alive. Sasha would never be away this long and not contact her family. But even if she's dead, I want her to have a proper burial," she said with tears in her eyes.

After Alberta left, Nana put her tarot cards away. She took a deep breath and picked up her phone. It had to be done.

"Sheriff Fisher."

"Sheriff, it's Nana. I just did a reading for the mother of the missing girl, Sasha. I'm sorry to inform you I think I know where her body is," Nana said almost in a whisper.

"I'll be right there," he said and hung up.

She looked over at Moro who had been sleeping.

"Moro, this is a sad day."

He just looked at her with his sad eyes and barked. Then he went back to sleep.

Shortly after, Sheriff Fisher arrived at the campground. She told him to take a seat, and then after he was given a Cafécito, he took out his notebook, and waited for Nana to tell her story.

"Alberta, Sasha's mother came by to ask for a reading. I agreed because I too wanted to find out what had happened to her daughter," Nana said.

She rubbed her hands together before she continued.

"As I was reading the cards, in addition to what they told me, I felt dread. There was an overwhelming sensation of grief. I knew then that Sasha was dead. When I was doing the reading, I could see the woods, a path, and then an abandoned cottage. It looks like it's falling apart. You will find her body buried behind the building by the large oak tree."

"Are you certain?"

"Yes. Her body is there. I'm sorry I can't pinpoint her exact location, but hopefully knowing that she's by an abandoned cottage will narrow down the search."

"Trust me, this is more than we had. I'll take it. Thank you very much."

———

S heriff Fisher stood and hugged Nana taking her by surprise. He walked out of the caravan and softly closed the door behind him.

———

"M i vida, what do you want to do today?"

"Déjame pensar. I have to think. Why don't we head into that small town we've been hearing about. We can explore the shops, walk around, and then find a cozy place for lunch?"

"You know I love you," Eddie said as he grabbed his wife and kissed her.

"Yes, I do Eddie. *You* are my prince charming," Juana replied with a smile.

"Eddie, can we invite Nana?"

"Of course. Let's plan on leaving in ten minutes."

"Perfecto. I'll head over to her caravan to see if she wants to join us. I'll be back." She kissed him, and walked out the door.

Juana walked next door to Nana's place and was about to knock on the door when Sheriff Fisher walked out.

"Good day to you," Juana said with a smile.

"Juana, so very nice to see you."

"I just stopped by to invite Nana to join us on an excursion, but if she's busy…"

"No, I'm leaving. Don't let me interfere. We'll talk later Nana," he said as he walked to his cruiser.

"Is everything alright Nana?" Juana asked concerned.

"Yes, everything is fine. So, tell me about this excursion," she said with a smile.

Nana decided to keep the real reason Sheriff Fisher was there to herself until she could confirm her suspicions were correct. When Juana finished explaining what they had planned, Nana decided it was exactly what she needed.

"Count me in, sounds like fun."

"Hay que bueno, we leave in ten minutes."

"Perfecto, I'll be ready. Gracias."

When the time came Nana told Moro to make sure no one came into the caravan. She was starting to feel somewhat vulnerable. Going on an excursion with Juana and Eddie was just what she needed.

She locked the door of her caravan, and walked to the

truck. Once everyone was settled, Eddie started the engine and off they went.

The rest of the day was spent walking around Main Street, window shopping, and chatting away … until Juana noticed through a cozy couple through the window.

Nudging her slightly, she whispered to Nana.

"Look who appears to be very happy right now," she said as she pointed to the window in the restaurant across the street.

When Nana looked, sure enough, there, were Sally and Mario acting very cozy. She wondered if this had been going on while Leonardo was alive or if this budding relationship started after his death. Nana was curious to find out more, but she couldn't just go up to them and ask.

"Nana, Nana!"

"Sorry, I was thinking about something I have to do tomorrow," she replied to Juana hoping she hadn't noticed her staring at Sally and Mario.

"Well, I'm hungry and that restaurant looks amazing."

She turned around and noticed Eddie had stayed behind. So, she waved at him to get his attention and then pointed to the restaurant.

"Eddie, let's have lunch at that restaurant across the street. I'll get us a table," she yelled out as she grabbed Nana's arm to cross the street.

"Está bien. I'll be right there. Dame un minute. Please just give me a minute," he replied as he walked into one of the boutique stores.

Juana and Nana walked into the restaurant, and spoke to the hostess.

"Good afternoon, would you like a table?"

"Yes, please. Party of three," Juana replied as she nudged Nana.

Nana had noticed that the couple was very chummy, lost in their own world. Juana, devious as she was asked to be seated close to the window. That would put them very near Sally and Mario.

As the hostess showed them their table, they were all silent. Sally and Mario still hadn't noticed them.

"Hey, Sally, Mario?" Juana said loud enough to interrupt them.

Startled they both sat back. Sally's face grew red, while Mario just continued to look at his menu. Nana watched all of this without saying a word.

"This is our first time at this restaurant. Is the food any good here?" Juana asked with a smile.

"Um, yes. The food is very good. We just ran into each other and decided to try out the restaurant," she replied looking nervous.

Nana noticed they hadn't touched their plates.

"Great. Do you recommend anything in particular?" Juana just kept on asking questions rattling them.

That's when Sally looked down at her plate and realized her answer didn't match her actions. It was obvious they hadn't eaten anything yet. That's when she sat straight and looked directly, first at Juana and then at Nana, and spoke.

"Well, well. What a pleasant surprise to see you here. If you'll excuse us, we need to finish our meal before it gets cold," she replied.

There were daggers in her eyes as she spoke. She turned around, and grabbed a bite of her food.

"That was awkward," Juana whispered.

"I think being caught was not in their plans," Nana replied.

"Ladies, let's enjoy our lunch," Eddie said.

Nana and Juana looked at each other and nodded, but Nana kept an eye on them for the rest of lunch. Not once did they hold hands again.

Just then Eddie arrived and without realizing what was happening approached Sally and Mario.

"Hey guys, nice to see you hear. How's the food?"

"It's great," Mario answered.

"Thanks."

Eddie answered and sat down.

Sally and Mario finished their lunch quickly and left.

Juana asked out loud what Nana had been thinking.

"Wonder how long that's been going on?"

"¿Verdad? I wonder too."

"Ladies, no sleuthing. No se metan. Do not get involved. Let's just enjoy our lunch," Eddie said as he looked at each of them.

"Fine," Juana said as she shrugged her shoulders.

"So, do we have time to stop at a few other stores before we need to head back?" Nana asked.

"Yes, of course," Eddie replied.

The rest of the lunch they spent talking about the area and how friendly everyone was. They soon forgot about Sally and Mario.

By the time they returned to the campground it was almost nightfall. Nana thanked Eddie and Juana and went to her caravan. Moro was patiently waiting to be walked.

"Let's go. Sorry I got back so late. We lost track of time," she said to Moro as she patted his head.

I was sleeping most of the time.

"Que bueno. I was feeling guilty for leaving you alone for so long."

No worries, Matilda kept me entertained.

"Hay Dios mio. I can only imagine," Nana giggled, "you know, I'm actually getting used to her hanging around. She does keep us entertained."

So, anything interesting happened today?

Nana looked around to make sure no one was around before answering him. She realized that not many people used the trail which was surprising since it was so beautiful.

"Yes. As a matter of fact, we saw Sally and Mario very

cozy in a restaurant. We surprised them and it was obvious they were rattled. They rushed to finish their meals and left."

WOW!

"Me lo dices. Very interesting indeed. Anyway, I've been thinking, from the information I was able to gather at the party, that Beth Blackguard is someone we need to look into. Did you know that many years ago, while she was married, she had an affair with Leonardo?"

Como sabes? How did you find out?

"I read her mind. She kept thinking over and over again that had she not broken off the relationship, maybe they'd be married and he wouldn't have been killed."

Nana was able to find out that Beth had dated Leonardo for over a year. She broke it off when he began insisting that she choose between him and her husband. At that point she wasn't ready to leave her husband, and chose instead to end the relationship with Leonardo.

As far as Beth was concerned, no one knew about them. It seemed lately she had been trying to win him back, telling him she'd regretted ever letting him go, and would he give her another chance. She knew the relationship between him and Sally was not on solid ground.

So, you're thinking that because he wouldn't consider going back to her, she became enraged and killed him?

"That's what it's looking like. I just have to confirm a few more details before I can say anything to Sheriff Fisher."

Just then, she saw Bill approaching them from the other side of the path.

"Nana, Moro, how are you both doing? Out late, aren't you?"

"It's quiet around this time and Moro can roam easier with fewer people around. What brings you out here so far from the campground?"

"I enjoy walking the trail often. It allows me the opportunity to think."

Nana tried to read his mind, but this time there was nothing there. Either he was purposely blocking her or he just wasn't thinking about anything in particular. Darn, she really was hoping to get a reading from him.

Maybe that anger she had experienced before was temporary. Could she have been wrong about him? It was difficult to tell with Bill. Especially, now that he kept his thoughts so guarded.

Maybe he wasn't as dangerous as she originally imagined, she thought to herself.

"Would you like company on your walk?"

"Well, we were actually heading back. If you want to join us…"

"Wonderful," he replied with a smile.

See, that's what she was talking about … that smile seemed forced. It was hard to pinpoint the emotion he caused in her, but it definitely wasn't pleasant.

"Have you heard anything new about the investigation?" Bill asked.

"Which one?"

"Actually, I was asking about Leonardo, but have you heard anything about the missing camper?"

"Nothing new on Leonardo. I believe the Sheriff may have some leads, but I haven't heard anything new. As to the missing camper, there's reason to believe she may be dead and her body is somewhere near."

Bill remained silent for a moment before responding.

"What makes you think the camper is dead?"

Now, she needed to tread carefully. Should she say she saw her in a tarot card reading? Or should she say that it was what she'd overheard? Either way if he was Leonardo's killer or had anything to do with the camper, she was putting herself in direct danger. She didn't think he had anything to do with being hit over the head, but again she wasn't certain.

Moro cautioned her, but she felt she needed to see his reaction.

"I think the person that killed the camper is the same person that hit me over the head," she said.

She watched Bill closely to see his reaction. For a split second she saw him twitch. She knew it, he had something to do with either Leonardo or the camper. Now, all she had to do was prove it.

"Who would do such a terrible thing?" Bill replied appearing concerned.

"No se, I really don't know who could be so callous as to hurt someone and think they can get away with it. It's probably someone who just came upon the campground. It couldn't be anyone we know, right?" she asked him not really expecting an answer.

Now, Bill seemed to relax.

"You're probably correct. Maybe we should hang out together just in case this person tries anything again," he suggested.

"You are so kind. I have Moro, but you know what? I'll think about it. It can't hurt to have someone else looking after you," she said with a smile.

I don't trust him.

Nana nodded.

I'm thinking he had something to do with Leonardo's death more than the camper. Now, we have Beth and Bill to consider. We still need to figure out who could have killed Sasha and why?

Woof.

"Moro seems happy."

"Yes, he's always happy when we return to the campground."

Bill accompanied her all the way to her caravan.

"Thank you for letting me walk with you both. It was nice spending time with you. We should get together for a proper outing soon," Bill suggested.

"Gracias, Bill," she replied ignoring his suggestion.

"Well, I guess I'll see you later." Bill said as he waved goodbye.

What motive could he have to kill Leonardo?

"That's what has me confused. I think I need to focus back on Beth. She had motive if she tried to get back with Leonardo and he refused her. Maybe she even knew about his inheritance. Wouldn't that be interesting if that was the case?"

All valid questions.

"I need to check more into Beth's relationship and what she has known about Leonardo now."

Have you thought of asking Matilda to do a little spying? It's easier for her than me.

"I'm not sure I want to involve her in this …"

Are you talking about me?

"Matilda, so nice to see you. Actually, we were talking about potential killers," Nana knew that would catch her attention.

Killers, how exciting.

Well, that's interesting. That's not the response expected. Crazy woman.

"I'm planning on finding out if Beth is the one who killed Leonardo. There's some new evidence that has come to light which may serve to be very interesting. If she doesn't work out, there is always Bill. He is hiding something, and although he doesn't look like a killer, you never know."

Well, I can snoop around for you, if you want?

See, told ya.

Taking a deep breath, she thought, about the alternative, and figured what harm could it do?

"Fine. I don't want you doing anything except just observing. Go over to Beth's RV and see if she's doing anything suspicious. Or better yet, see if she mentions Leonardo in any way. You can't read her thoughts, but if she says anything out loud, let me know."

Sounds like a plan. This is going to be fun, Matilda said and disappeared with a poof.

"Por Dios. Matilda murder is not fun," Nana said out loud even though she was already gone.

Later that night she decided that the next morning she'd approach Beth to see if she could do another tarot card reading. She always walked up to the food truck to get breakfast. *That's the perfect spot to approach her*, Nana thought as she dozed off to sleep.

❖

———

❖

Chapter 7

❖

First thing the next morning, Nana sent Juana a text.

Amiga, are you up for some sleuthing?

Immediately Juana replied.

Absolutely! What do you need?

Come over when you have a minute and I'll explain everything.

Within ten minutes, Juana was knocking on the door. Nana smiled as she let her inside.

Suddenly the temperature dropped.

"Nana, you really need to get this checked out," Juana said as she waved her hand around the room.

"Someone is coming to check on the draft, but it doesn't really bother me."

She shrugged her shoulders. Knowing Nana, it really didn't bother her and there was no changing that.

Matilda was talking at the same time as Juana and at one point Nana screamed.

"Basta!"

Juana stopped talking and looked alarmed. Not wanting

to say a ghost was driving her crazy she sent Moro an apology before blaming the whole incident on him.

"Oh, sorry Juana. It was Moro, he kept twitching," she said not looking directly at him, worried he would make her laugh.

Have some fun on my account.

"Sorry," this time, it was meant for Moro.

"Oh, I thought I had said something wrong."

"No, Juana it was not you. So, before you continue let me just tell you what I'm thinking," she said as she looked at Juana and Matilda.

They both remained quiet.

"It has been brought to my attention that Beth may have a connection to Leonardo, and I want to explore that somewhat. So, I thought if you accompany me to the food truck... she's always there and I could somehow encourage her to do another reading with me. Maybe even say something like, we were interrupted at the party and I couldn't finish. Hopefully, she won't remember that it's not the case."

Juana was nodding, agreeing with the plan.

That's a great idea, especially since the only thing I got from watching her was that she definitely misses Leonardo.

"Perfecto. Alright, let's head out to the food truck, and hope she's there like she always is around this time."

They walked in silence until they approached the food truck. Sure enough, there was Beth in line placing an order. Nana turned to Juana.

"So, we will just have a casual conversation about tarot card readings and crystal balls. Just follow my lead. I'm certain you'll be able to follow along easily."

She patted her friend's arm.

Walking up to the line, Nana and Juana said good morning to everyone. Beth seemed to be in better spirits than she had been several days ago, and after placing her order, seated herself at an empty table.

Perfect, thought Nana, *we can go join her as soon as we place our orders.*

Once they were done, Nana walked towards Beth, Juana followed.

"Beth, do you mind if we sit here while we wait for our food?"

She hesitated before answering. To avoid her saying no, Juana interjected.

"Don't worry, we won't bother you. Not everyone is a morning person," she said, laughing.

"Of course, you're more than welcome to sit. And, don't worry. In fact, I am a morning person," she said with a smile.

Both ladies sat and eventually Nana started up the conversation.

"So, wasn't it fun having your tarot cards read. It was definitely great fun for me."

"Yes, I can't wait to have them read again. Maybe next time you can also do the crystal ball."

Nana was glad Juana was getting into character. She was actually doing a great job.

"I'm just sorry, so many people had to have their sessions cut-off, or not even having a session."

Juana picked up quickly where Nana was taking this conversation.

"What are you going to do about those people Nana?"

"Well, as a matter of fact, I was thinking of offering them a free session. It's not their fault it was canceled."

"That's a great idea," Juana replied as she looked at Beth, "Right Beth? That's so generous of Nana."

"Actually, Beth you are one of those people that I was going to ask. Would you like a new reading as your session was interrupted?"

Beth debated whether she should, but figured at this point what could it hurt, especially since she thought Nana was probably a fake.

"Sure. That sounds like fun. When do you want to do the session?"

"The sooner the better. How about in an hour? Come over to my caravan and we can do a reading inside. It'll be private," Nana replied with a smile.

"Great, thanks," Beth replied.

Just then Beth's name was called. She stood and walked over to retrieve her food. Before she left, she turned around and faced Nana and Juana.

"See you in a bit Nana," she said as she waved at them.

"That went quite well, don't you think?"

"Yes, it was way too easy. But I'm glad she fell for it. Now, all I have to do is somehow prove that she killed Leonardo."

"Nana, you're relentless," Juana chuckled.

When their names were called, they decided to stay and eat there. Juana had mentioned that Eddie had left very early in the morning to play golf and would not return for still another few hours.

They chatted about camping, living in the campground, and how in spite of the things that had happened, how happy they were to be there.

"I really like living here. Everything is within arm's reach. For the most part it's drama free, and I've made some great friends. I really do think I'm going to enjoy living here for a full year," Nana said with a smile.

"I'm so glad you said that, because we are really enjoying ourselves and can't imagine leaving any time before our year is up."

When they got back to Nana's caravan, Juana asked if she needed her to stick around. Nana assured her nothing was going to happen and thanked her for helping her with their little role play. They hugged and Juana left.

Nana grabbed her tarot cards, a glass of water, incense, and decided the crystal ball would come in handy too, even if just for show. She prepared everything she needed including lighting the incense.

By the time Beth arrived, the caravan had a calming atmosphere about it that would put the most nervous person at ease.

Beth entered and looked around.

"You know, I've never been inside your caravan. It's actually stunning. What beautiful rich colors you have here, and look at these details, just beautiful."

"Thank you, Beth. Now, if you'll have a seat right here, we can get started."

Nana proceeded to shuffle the cards while she spoke.

"Since I feel bad that we had to cancel your session I'm going to give you a treat. Besides using the tarot cards for a reading, I'll also use the crystal ball which sometimes can offer a better result."

Now, Beth was a little uncertain about the whole thing. Nana was sure Beth was about to back out.

"So, to put your mind at ease in case you have doubts. Here, can you see how the crystal ball is clear? When I rub it, if it was working you would see a fog or something," Nana said as she rubbed the crystal ball.

Her fingers began to tingle and she prayed that this time Beth could not see the fog. No one had seen it before, so there was no reason she should. Sure enough, Beth put her face almost up to the crystal ball and then retreated.

"Nothing happened."

"Exactly. It's really more for show, but let's give it a go anyway. Think of what you want to ask and I'll throw some things out that may or may not be helpful. Let's begin."

Nana continued to rub the crystal ball until the first image appeared.

"I see you taking a long trip. Although, something is holding you back. There is someone you keep thinking about that is invading your every thought, even when you're asleep," Nana said and looked at Beth who was now stoic.

So, she continued.

"This person is a man from your past. You never stopped caring for him and have regret your decision of letting him go. Oh … I see," she let the words linger.

"What did you see? What does it say?" she asked in a desperate voice.

At that point Beth started to cry.

"Are you alright?"

"Yes, I'm sorry. Please continue."

"Let me try again… I see the letter L. Does that mean anything to you?"

This time Beth started crying uncontrollably. Nana waited as she knew she had hit a chord. She stood and brought over the tissue box handing a tissue to Beth. She nodded as she blew her nose and wiped her eyes with a second tissue.

"I believe it's a man, a man you have come to realize you are in love with. There have been other men, but they never made you feel like this L person did. However, I'm sorry to say it's too late. I don't know why, just that this relationship cannot be. Wait, I see an argument. Did you recently have a fight with this person?"

Now Beth gasped. But instead of answering she nodded. Nana was so close, but she couldn't push it, it needed to appear as if she truly was getting a vision. Just at that moment Matilda appeared and Nana smiled at her. Beth noticed immediately the drop in temperature and looked around desperately to find the source. Nana continued.

"I see there was an argument. Did it get out of hand? Did something happen?" Nana asked.

"Why is it so cold in here all of a sudden?"

"I believe it's probably somebody who has passed on that is attached to you. They have come to send you a message. Would you like me to try and communicate with them?"

"Oh, can it be Leo? Yes, please." Beth sounded desperate.

"You did say Leo? Is that right?"

Beth nodded yes.

"Alright, Leo is that you here?" Nana asked while looking at Matilda who at this point was dancing around the room. Nana tried as best as she could to not start laughing. She waited a few seconds before continuing.

"I believe he is here, your Leo. He says he loved you, but wants to know why you tried to hurt him?"

Beth abruptly stood knocking over the chair and ran out without bothering to shut the door.

"Well, that went well *Leo*," Nana said to Matilda and Moro as one laughed and the other barked.

"I should go check on her. I'll be right back."

Nana approached Beth's RV, and as she was about to knock on the door, she heard drawers being banged shut, then footsteps, then the sounds of someone searching for something.

Finally, Nana heard footsteps approaching the front door. This was her chance to appear as if she had just arrived.

Knocking she called out.

"Beth, are you alright?"

Her voice grew near as the door knob turned.

"I'm fine Nana. I really can't talk right now."

From what Nana could see, drawers were laying on the floor, as were papers. She did notice a suitcase on the bed.

"Alright, dear. I'm sorry if I upset you," Nana said as she took one step down.

"Everything will be alright now. You don't have to worry about me anymore," she said, and with that shut the door and locked it.

Nana stepped away from the RV and called Sheriff Fisher.

"Sheriff Fisher."

"Sheriff, it's Nana. You need to come out to the campground immediately. I just had a session with Beth. I made her think that Leonardo was in the room when the temperature dropped. It was a hunch and obviously it paid off. I learned they had a relationship in the past. It appears she must have regretted letting him go. I believe she may have tried to kill him. Now, she's in her RV which looks like it's been ransacked and there's a suitcase on the bed. I think she's going to flee. The one thing that concerns me is what she just said to me in a very calm voice," Nana repeated Beth's last words.

"I'm on my way. Don't let her leave."

Por Dios. She ran back to her caravan and called Moro.

"I need you to help me guard Beth's RV. She can't leave until Sheriff Fisher arrives. You Matilda, you come too and stick very close to her if she tries to flee."

Nana ran back to the RV with Moro and Matilda in tow. She could hear Beth inside. Nana stood outside the door blocking her exit.

Just then Sheriff Fisher and another patrol car arrived and parked in front of her RV blocking her exit.

Nana nodded and stepped out of the way.

"Beth Blackguard, this is Sheriff Fisher. Open this door."

He had to repeat himself several times and bang on her door twice more before she slowly opened the door. When she did, she was holding a gun to her head.

"Put the gun down!" Sheriff Fisher ordered her.

"No, I don't want to live without him. It's all my fault that he's dead."

Her hand was shaking while she spoke. Nana moved further out of the way. She knew what a crazed woman with a gun was capable of doing.

"Please, let me have the gun, and tell me what is going on," Sheriff Fisher's tone was calm and almost a whisper.

Beth blinked several times, then threw herself on the floor. Sheriff Fisher retrieved the gun before it discharged.

He and the officer walked inside and closed the door.

Nana didn't want to leave, so she sent Matilda to let her know what was going on.

"Tell me what is going on, and why you think ending your life would solve anything?" Sheriff Fisher asked after he helped her get up and sat her down on one of the chairs.

"Don't you see? I love Leonardo. If I hadn't ended our relationship all of those years ago, he wouldn't have had to marry Sally. He should have been with me. I killed him, and now the only way to be with him is if I also die."

"How did you kill him?"

"With peanuts. I had just been eating peanuts and still had some on my fingers. Leo was allergic to peanuts."

"Go, on." Sheriff Fisher encouraged her to continue.

"I came into the RV when I saw Henry leave and started kissing him. I told him I still loved him. Then he said he loved me too. He was going to divorce Sally, and finally marry me."

Sheriff Fisher waited patiently for her to tell her story.

"I was so happy that we were finally going to be together. He told me he'd see me after his massage. When Henry left for the second time I waited and waited. At first, I thought he had changed his mind and I was devastated. Then when I had decided, I was going to confront him, Sally started screaming at the top of her lungs. I was paralyzed … I couldn't move. This time I was really devastated, and then when I heard he had died of peanut poisoning I knew I had killed him."

Sheriff Fisher didn't think her having her hands all over his body and kissing him would cause him to die, but he was not taking any chances. He stood and between him and the officer they helped her to her feet. While he was reading her, her rights, he handcuffed her. Once he was done, he walked her out of the RV.

Nana moved aside when they came outside. She tried to read Beth's mind, but all she was getting was *I'm so sorry my love, please forgive me.*

The campers that were outside stood in silence as she was ushered away. Nana noticed Sally was looking out the window of her RV, but quickly closed the curtains.

Word spread like wildfire throughout the campground. Valdez came around and made an announcement on the PA for everyone to meet at the Main House for an update on what was happening.

Everyone attended the meeting. It was standing room only. He approached Sally first and told her that Sheriff Fisher had arrested the person responsible for Leonardo's death. Then he addressed the crowd.

"Folks, I just wanted to let you know that you can all rest easy now as Sheriff Fisher has arrested the person responsible for Leonardo's death. This person is in custody as we speak, so you can relax. Once Sally has decided on a date, we will have a celebration of life for him. Further information will be provided soon. Please don't ask me any questions, as I only know an arrest has been made, not who was arrested. Thank you, and please go about your business and enjoy the grounds," he said to the crowd as he set the microphone down.

Valdez walked up to Eddie, Juana, and Nana.

"Thank God that's all over."

"It's not," Nana said.

"What do you mean it's not? An arrest has been made."

Valdez had a look of panic. He was concerned his camp-ground had already been tarnished, and he just wanted this to be over.

"Yes, that true. But the amount of peanut she transferred to him wouldn't have caused him to die. The killer is still out there, mark my words," Nana said as she turned around and walked out of the building.

❖

❖

Chapter 8

❖

B ack at the station, Beth was inconsolable. She kept crying and repeating over and over again how she had killed him, and all she wanted was to join him. She didn't want to live without his Leonardo.

Sheriff Fisher was confused at the turn of events. He hadn't even been aware that they'd known each other from before. As a matter of fact, he'd been told she had a relationship with a guy named Reginald.

After a while, he tried again to speak with Beth.

"How are you feeling?"

This time she looked at him with such sadness, it concerned him that she might be indeed suicidal.

"I'm better."

"I wanted to ask you to tell me about your relationship with Leonardo Jones. Start at the beginning."

For the next hour Beth told Sheriff Fisher how they first met. How they ended up having a relationship, and how it had ended. She had not seen him in a very long time until he showed up with his wife Sally one day at one of the trips organized by the Miami Coastal Caravan Club.

At that point she'd been in a relationship with someone she wasn't really interested in, it was just a fling. Once she saw Leonardo again, she immediately dropped the other man.

"Did he start seeing you after you both ran into each other?"

"Yes, and no. He was faithful to that stupid woman who didn't even care about him. Did you know she's been having an affair with Mario while she was still married to Leonardo? I heard they'd been seeing each other for over a year," she spat as she said the last words.

It was obvious she was disgusted with the entire situation.

"Go on."

"Anyway, on those occasions when she would disappear, Leonardo and I would take long walks on the trail. We had started to spend more and more time together. No one in the campground knew about us. We were very discreet. No, we didn't sleep together. He wanted to be free of Sally before he started up with me again."

"So, you knew Leonardo back in the day, and recently started to spend time with him again?" Nana wanted to make certain she understood the relationship.

"Yes. Leonardo had grown disillusioned with her blatant cheating. The last time we spoke he said he had made a decision to leave Sally. He even called his attorney to change his will," she answered as she sighed.

"So, what happened?"

"We had talked the day before about meeting after his massage. I was bored sitting around outside my RV eating a peanut butter sandwich and licking my fingers when I saw Henry walk out of the RV without his table or bag. I figured he was going to come right back. So, I dared myself to go in there, kiss him and run out."

"And?"

"I did just that. I ran inside while he was standing by the table covered only in a towel. I grabbed his face, kissed him all over, and told him how much I loved him. He kissed me back passionately and then stopped. I assumed it was because he was afraid Henry would return and catch us, so before he could say anything I kissed him again, and said I'd be waiting for him. I then ran out of the RV just before Henry returned."

Beth started crying again.

"Did you know he was allergic to peanuts?"

"Yes, of course. But I wasn't thinking. All I wanted was to spend time with Leonardo. I was finally happy, and I couldn't wait to share my life with him. Then everything changed in an instant. Now, I'm all alone and all I want is to be with him."

This time she lay her head in her lap and rocked back and forth. Sheriff Fisher called one of the female officers and asked her to check her thoroughly for any hidden weapons because he believed she was suicidal, then place her in a private cell.

Sheriff Fisher placed a call to the coroner's office to find out if Beth's kissing Leonardo could have killed him.

"Yes. In fact, if he was highly allergic her transfer of saliva could cause swelling of the lips or throat, hives and even wheezing."

"Thank you, Doc., It seems we can close the file on the case of Leonardo Jones."

Sheriff Fisher called in his deputies and announced with Ms. Blackguard's confession they could now mark the case closed. He would send all of the information to the District Attorney's office in the morning and it would be up to them how they wanted to charge her. He decided he should visit Mrs. Jones and let her know what had happened.

Before he could leave, Nana stormed into the station. She walked right up to him and told him not to close the case.

"Beth Blackguard is not your killer. Please don't close the case."

"Nana, I appreciate your concern, but we have a confession. I even confirmed with the coroner's office that her kissing him and placing her hands all over his body would have caused the symptoms he exhibited."

"Yes, I know all that, but I'm telling you that she is not the killer. She may have kissed him and exacerbated the situation, but she is *not* the killer."

"What makes you say that? What proof do you have that Beth did not kill Leonardo?"

Nana debated whether to tell him about her ability to see ghosts or if she should make something up. Now, Leonardo had not appeared to her, so she couldn't actually ask him who killed him, but every bone in her body told her that Beth is not the killer.

"Give me twenty-four hours to bring the killer to you. That's all I ask of you, please."

Sheriff Fisher mulled over what she was saying, and his gut was telling him she was telling the truth. He wavered over whether to just accept Beth's confession which would mean that she would probably be sent to jail. But what if she thought she killed him, but in reality, all she actually did was give him in haste a kiss. If that was the case, then there was no intent. That meant that someone else had deliberately killed him. Taking a deep breath, he said a silent prayer and hoped he wasn't making a mistake.

"Alright, Nana you have twenty-four hours to prove that Beth Blackguard did not intentionally kill Leonardo."

"Thank you," she replied and rushed out of the station.

She got in her truck, turned on the ignition and peeled out of the parking lot. Luckily at that particular moment, there were no patrolmen outside. Otherwise, they would've given her a ticket.

When she arrived back at the campground, she went

directly to her caravan. She parked her truck, turned off the ignition, locked the car and ran inside her caravan locking the door behind her.

She immediately went for the crystal ball and called out to Matilda. The moment she appeared Nana told her what she needed.

"Matilda, I need to make sure I'm doing this correctly. Now more than ever, I need this to work. I have to prove that Beth did not intentionally try to kill Leonardo. I believe with everything I hold dear that the real killer is still out there."

What do you need?

"I'm going to concentrate once I have rubbed the crystal ball. I need you to see if for you it remains clear or if you too can see something. If you can see something, then I need you to pay attention to make sure I don't miss anything."

I'm here for you.

Nana took out the crystal ball and carefully set it on the table. She decided she'd burn incense to help her concentrate. When she felt she was ready, she asked it to show her who killed Leonardo.

Slowly the fingers began to tingle, and little by little, the crystal ball started to fog. Then when it was completely covered in fog, the images started to appear.

Out loud Nana narrated what she saw as Matilda sat there nodding her agreement.

"I see Beth happily walking into Leonardo's RV. Now, I see her smiling as she walks out and turns left towards her own RV. She doesn't look like someone who just committed murder," Nana said as she looked at Matilda.

I agree. Keep looking.

Nana closed her eyes this time for a second, and then opened them again, and looked directly into the ball.

"I see Henry running out of the RV ... I think he's going to his car. I see him returning. I can hear him talking to Leonardo."

Nana stopped.

"That's it. I heard Henry talking to Leonardo. That means there's no way Beth killed him if he was talking to Henry. Something else happened from the time Henry returned and then left for the last time."

Matilda bent over the crystal ball to make sure what she was seeing was accurate. There in black and white popped up the faces of Linda, Bill, and Sally.

"Muy interesante. I knew it had to be someone else. Linda, Bill and Sally, wow. Está bien. We have work to do," Nana said as she rubbed the crystal ball again.

This time she didn't feel the tingle in her fingers and the fog began to dissipate. She knew that meant the crystal ball had done what it needed to do, and now it was up to Nana to figure out what everything meant.

"I need to do a reading for those three. It can't hurt to just show up and offer them a reading. To Sally I'll say it's to make sure that Beth remains behind bars for killing her husband. With Linda, I can say it's … I don't know yet. And, finally Bill. He's going to be the most difficult as I don't think he will be that easy to convince."

What do we know so far?

"Well, Moro, I know that Linda has been flirting with Mario, who has shown her he's interested. That means he is either using Sally or using Linda. Then there's Miriam and her husband. At first, I thought I needed to keep an eye on them, but as it turns out they had nothing to do with either killing Leonardo or the missing camper."

So, we can eliminate those two?

"Yes, they're just a passionate couple who seem to be in the clear."

We're doing well so far. By the way, I'm having a hard time wrapping my head around Linda and Mario, but still interesting.

"Right? Están loco. Anyway, then there's Bill and Sally. I still think there is something up with Bill. Maybe he's interested in Sally and he killed Leonardo so that he could finally have her to himself. But she seems very cozy with Mario. I don't really think she's interested in Bill, unless it's a one-way obsession meaning he is the only one that interested in Sally, but she is not interested in him."

What about Sally?

"Sally, is a very interesting sort. She is obviously not bothered by her husband's death. It only been a few weeks and she's already openly involved with Mario. If rumors are correct, she's been seeing him since long before Leonardo was killed. Could she have killed him to be with Mario? Possibly. Did she have an accomplice? Mostly likely."

Nana was now confident that she could focus on Linda, Mario, Bill, and Sally.

Nana, what about Olga? You had originally thought maybe she was someone of interest.

"I realized she's just infatuated, but of no concern to us. No, I have my four suspects. Now I have to get to work."

For the rest of the day, she worked out the different scenarios for how she could approach her suspects to do a reading, without them becoming suspicious. Satisfied she was ready, she decided to join the other members by the campfire. The music was already playing and someone had brought drinks.

Nana changed into a pair of jeans, a long sleeve white shirt, and grabbed a jean jacket from her closet. For shoes she debated between tennis shoes and flip flops. *Fine*, she thought to herself. She realized she couldn't just show up in flip flops.

"Moro, let's go hang out with the club members. I need a break from all of the sleuthing," she said as she grabbed her glass and headed towards the campfire.

"Nana, so happy you could join us," Miriam said with a smile as she patted the empty space next to her.

Smiling Nana greeted everyone as she made her way to her seat. People were dancing and drinking, and they looked like they didn't have a care in the world. Of course, Nana couldn't help but be observant. She watched Linda and her beau, she watched Sally and Mario, and then there was Bill in the corner drinking, but not participating.

"¿Nana, estás bien?"

"Si, Juana gracias. I'm just watching everyone having so much fun and it feels good."

"Verdad? Right? This is great. I'm so glad we came out tonight. By the way, Eddie says it's up to me when we should renew our vows. I'm thinking we wait until we are home and do a small party at the beach. What do you think?"

"That sounds wonderful. Perfecto."

"Bueno, when I'm ready to start planning can I count on you to help?" Juana asked in a hopeful tone.

"Claro que si! Of course. You don't have to even ask. It would be my pleasure to organize such a special event," Nana said with a smile.

"Ladies, no more gossiping. Now, let's dance," Eddie encouraged them to come to the dance area as he made some silly moves.

Everyone laughed. Nana and Juana stood and walked out to the dance area and started dancing. Soon Miriam and Pedro joined, as did Linda and her beau. Before long, they were all up and dancing. Even Bill joined for a bit. After several songs Nana was ready to rest her feet. As she looked around, she noticed Sally, Mario, and Bill were gone.

Darn. I lost an opportunity to speak with them. Oh well, maybe it was for the best. I can't come across as being too pushy, she thought to herself.

The rest of the night was spent telling jokes, drinking, and dancing the night away. Right before going back to her caravan, Nana decided to walk Moro. The easiest walk was down the trail.

"Not too far tonight alright? I'm really tired and need to

get some rest before I can tackle these suspects in the morning."

Sure, I'll be quick.

Moro ran ahead of her. Suddenly, he started to bark repeatedly and Nana became alarmed. She ran towards the sound of the barking until she found Moro. He was standing close to what looked like a newly disturbed mound. When he realized she was near, he continued to dig until he found a finger.

At first, Nana was confused. She knew instantly Moro had found Sasha's body, but her vision was of the body in an abandoned cottage. How could then this be her body? Unless the killer moved her. But if that's the case, why?

"Stop. Let me call the Sheriff," Nana said as she took out her phone.

"Before you even say your name, it's Nana."

"You only call me when there's a problem. Tell me you didn't find another body?"

"Well ,..."

"What happened and where are you?" Now he sounded alarmed.

"Moro had been barking nonstop, and when I caught up to him, I noticed the area where he was digging had been recently disturbed. Then I saw a finger. I think it's Sasha."

"You know we got interrupted with another emergency before we could follow up on your tip. However, when we finally found the cottage you mentioned, and we searched the immediate area, we did find a spot where someone had been digging. If this is Sasha you found today, then I think someone moved the body."

"Hurry, I'm not sure we're alone here in the woods," she whispered.

"Stay on the phone with me," he said as he stood and grabbed his keys.

Sheriff Fisher yelled at the officers to follow him as he ran out of the station. Before long the campground was swarming with police officers.

The party ended abruptly when everyone realized that a body had been found. Quickly they retired to their RVs and caravans without protest. Nana stayed with Sheriff Fisher until it was confirmed it was the body of a woman. Because it had not been so long, the coroner was able to confirm based on some of the fibers found with the body, that it was indeed that of Sasha Tripp, the missing camper.

Valdez had just learned of the finding when he turned to his wife and said he'd probably have to close down the section for paying guests. Reporters will be invading the campground soon enough and only those friends and family will remain. At least he knew he didn't need the paying guests and that in turn would save him from losing the campground.

By the time Nana placed her head on her pillow she was exhausted. Moro jumped up on the bed and moved around until he settled at the foot of the bed. As she closed her eyes and fell into a deep sleep, she saw the person that stood in the distance watching her.

She tried to wake up, but it was fruitless. *No matter*, she thought to herself. She would just have to deal with it in the morning.

Chapter 9

The next morning Nana awoke feeing rather foggy. It was obvious she hadn't had enough sleep. Her body ached, and she was so tired she decided to stay in bed longer than normal. Eventually, knowing she couldn't hide in her caravan forever she slowly stretched and got out of bed. She went directly to shower, and there she stood letting the water hit her face for an extended time.

Finally, when the water started turning cold, she realized it was time to get out of the shower. She turned off the faucet, dried herself, and grabbed her bathrobe. Moro had been patiently waiting for her to let him out.

"Come on Moro, I trust you will be vigilant. Right before I fell asleep, I saw the person who was watching me last night. Of course, now for the life of me I can't remember who it was. Please be careful, and stay close to the caravan," she said as she opened the door for Moro.

She then locked the door and called out to Matilda. When she appeared, she looked upset.

"What's wrong Matilda?"

Nothing, I tend to get depressed every year when it gets close to the date I was murdered.

"Dios mio. I'm sorry for not asking you before if you knew when you were killed. So, today marks your anniversary?"

Tomorrow.

"Cuanto lo siento Matilda. I'm so very sorry."

That's alright. Did you need something from me?

"Yes, I wanted you to keep an eye out to make sure nothing happens to Moro. But if you're not up to it …"

Of course. You can count on me.

She disappeared before Nana could thank her again. Satisfied Moro was in good hands she returned to the bathroom to finish getting dressed. Just as she was finishing up Matilda returned letting Nana know that Moro was fine and waiting outside for her to open the door.

"Gracias."

Nana walked up to the door, unlocked it and there stood Moro patiently waiting. It was time to put her plan into motion. The first person she was going to see was Sally. But first she needed a Cafécito. So, she started out in the direction of the food truck, where she found Miriam, Pedro, Juana, and Eddie enjoying their breakfast.

"Buenos dias Nana," Miriam said.

"Buenos dias. How is everyone doing this morning?"

"We were talking about the body they found last night. We're still in shock," Pedro said.

"It's so sad that Moro was the one that found the body, but we are grateful that her family can now lay her to rest with a proper burial."

"Well, I hope this all gets resolved soon because we have new club members arriving within the next few days," Eddie said.

He was concerned about what might happen if there was still a killer roaming around the campground.

"Do you think the killer is still here? I assumed it was a

random person who wandered into the campground, but not one of our club members," Miriam said in a concerned voice.

"I think this will all be resolved soon," was all that Nana said.

Then she excused herself to go place her order, before she rejoined the group. They didn't mention anything further about the body, and Nana was grateful for that reprieve. Until her food arrived, they talked about areas they wanted to explore north of the campground, and how one of the members was organizing a ski trip to northern Vermont.

Nana was pleased that Pedro and Miriam seemed to be enjoying each other's company. When her name was called, she decided it was best to go back to the caravan. She told everyone she'd see them later and then walked back to her caravan as she took a bite of her tostada.

When she arrived back at her caravan, she noticed Sally standing outside her own RV. She figured this was as good a time as any.

"Sally, buenos dias. Good morning."

She seemed to have been crying.

"What's wrong?"

"Nothing. It's just been a very stressful couple of weeks."

"Well, I was going to come over later and offer to do a tarot card reading for you as I noticed these last few days you were not happy. If I may so bold as to ask, is everything alright with Mario?"

Sally looked at Nana for seemed like an eternity before responding.

"Mario … Mario seems to not be who I thought he was, and that makes me unhappy."

"So, a tarot card reading is just what you need. How about now?"

Sally was caught off guard and easily agreed. Nana knew this was going to be her only chance.

"Sit," she said to Sally, as she pointed towards the picnic table.

Sally did as she was told. Nana sat across from her. She placed her tostada and Cafécito on the table, and retrieved her tarot cards from her pocket. She shuffled them several times and then asked Sally to divide them in three piles. Once that was done, she then told her to make one pile.

Nana then took the cards from her and shuffled them once again. She then took the first card and turned it over. Cards never let her down.

The first card she pulled, was the Three of Swords. This card represents heartbreak. It is three swords stabbing a heart. In this instant Nana knew that it meant betrayal all around. She didn't say it out loud, but Sally betrayed Leonardo, and then Mario would betray her in the end.

"I see betrayal. There is much pain here, and I think it has nothing to do with your husband. It is a warning that you have caused pain to someone, and that in return you will experience pain and heartbreak."

Sally sat there silent without reacting.

Nana drew the next card. The Nine of Swords. This particular card represents the pain people carry with them. This card means you have done something wrong and you know it.

"I see again pain, but now it's more defined. I see anguish and guilt. I believe you've done something wrong, and you are quite aware of the significance of your actions. You need to change your ways because otherwise this overwhelming guilt that is weighing heavily on you, will destroy you.

The last card Nana drew was Death. Many clients think if this card is pulled, they will soon die, but that is not the case.

"Before I continue, I want you to know that my pulling this card does not mean you are going to die," Nana said as she looked at Sally before she continued with the reading.

"I see a relationship coming to an end. I also see a jar of

something. I can't quite make what's inside. Then I see an argument. These don't make any sense to me. Do they make sense to you?"

Nana knew she had struck a chord. Her instincts were correct. Now, to rattle her some more. Although, she usually picked only three cards, in this instance she needed one more to finish the job.

The final card is the Ten of Wands. This card means you have been defeated.

"This card represents defeat. Here I see things have been getting harder and harder for you. The end is near, and I don't mean death. The end of your burden is near. I see a police officer."

"Police?"

"Yes, that is strange right? Does any of this mean anything to you - jar, lotion, betrayal, burden, guilt ..." Nana didn't finish the sentence because at that moment it's as if Sally had flicked a switch.

"That conniving double crossing piece of ... He thought I didn't see him flirting with Linda. Does he think I'm stupid? I did all of this for him, and this is how he repays me."

Nana was about to put herself out there and prayed that it wouldn't backfire.

"The police know you poisoned Leonardo."

Sally rolled her head back and cackled.

"You can't prove anything you stupid, stupid woman," Sally continued to cackle.

It worked!

"Yes, I can."

Before she continued, she secretly dialed Sheriff Fisher's number and when she felt comfortable, he had answered the phone she continued. She wanted to make sure he could hear the entire conversation.

"You Sally made sure that Henry had to go back to his car for his lotion. He was very confused when he was ready to give Leonardo his massage and he realized he didn't have the jar he always uses, especially since that it was something that had never happened to him in the past."

Sally stared getting angrier and angrier. Nana continued.

"You purposely removed his jar so that he would have to go get a replacement, which you had made with peanut oil, knowing quite well that it would kill Leonardo."

"Beth confessed."

"Yes, that's true, but all she did was kiss him. That was not enough to have killed him. What killed him was the amount of lotion Henry used during this massage. The effects began to show as soon as Henry left the RV. But you knew that's what would happen."

"Again, you silly woman, you can't prove anything."

Nana continued.

"Aww, I see. Well, I have the name of the lab that created the lotion and the chemist you spoke with and met with can identify you as the person who ordered the lotion."

Suddenly, Sally stood and was about to attack Nana when Sheriff Fisher stormed into the area.

"Sally Jones, you are under arrest for the murder of your husband, Leonardo Jones," he said as he handcuffed her.

She was screaming obscenities as he dragged her to the cruiser. At that moment, Mario walked out of his RV and she locked eyes with him.

"You piece of crap. I did all of this for you and what did you do? You flirted with that, that woman. You were going to betray me. All this I did for you. I will kill you," she screamed as she tried to attack him.

She was held back, and forced her into the cruiser. As they drove away, she was still screaming.

Two days later, everyone learned that Sally ended up having a nervous breakdown. She rambled on and on about how she did it, and that it was all for Mario.

Beth returned to the campground and everyone welcomed

her with open arms. She thanked each and every one of them, and then went up to Nana and hugged her tightly.

"I heard you were responsible for finding the real killer. Thank you. You have no idea how grateful I am to know that I did not kill him. I will never forget Leo, but now I can rest easily knowing that I am not a killer, she whispered in Nana's ear.

She stepped back and squeezed Nana's hands.

"I'm so glad everything turned out the way it did. I knew you were not the killer. So, what are you planning next?"

"It's time to head home. I've missed my family. It's been too long, and now that Leo is gone, I need to be with family."

"Go in peace."

"Thank you."

By the next day, Beth had driven off the campground promising to return in the near future. Everyone waved as she drove off.

The rest of the day the club members stuck together chatting about what had happened, and how grateful they were that everything would go back to normal soon.

Nana wondered if she should bother insisting on a tarot card reading for Linda and Bill, but decided to let it go for now.

By the weekend new club members arrived. Valdez had organized several events to welcome the new campers. Nana tried her hand at skiing in the bunny slopes. Even after falling several times, she continued, not giving up. Soon, she'd be an expert. She even tried cross-country skiing. Nana was having the time of her life.

The more time she spent with Matilda, the more she realized she didn't want the ghost to leave. The good thing was that Matilda felt the same way. She was in no rush to find out who killed her. Besides she had waited this long, she could wait a little longer.

One November evening, a group of the club members

were sitting around a table in the Main House after one of the events when Juana mentioned Nana was a whiz at tarot card reading. Bill had been sitting across from her. He looked, but didn't comment. Soon, several were asking to have their cards read. Nana agreed.

One-by-one, she read their cards. She made sure to keep the information at a minimum so as to not freak anyone out, but still make it entertaining. Then it was Bill's turn, and she waited hoping he would let her read for him. Sure enough, he surprised her when he agreed.

She shuffled the cards and asked him to separate them into three piles, then she took the cards shuffled them once again, putting them all back into one pile.

The first card she drew was the Devil. This caught Bill's attention immediately.

"You know the Devil card is seen as a bad card, but in the tarot it's not necessarily a bad card," she said before continuing.

"Let's see what this card means for you. I see that there is something that sometimes takes control, and as much as you want to make it stop, you can't."

The next card Nana pulled was the Judgment card. This card wants you to stop and really examine the thoughts that are going through your mind. Its theme is of betrayal, and negativity.

"I see you are in constant turmoil. You must stop and think about what keeps nagging you. Before you can move forward, you need to step up and take responsibility for your actions."

Nana continued without missing a beat. The third card she pulled was the Nine of Swords.

"Finally, I see that there are negative thoughts controlling you. You have negative tendencies that are not good for you. You need to seek help before it's too late."

That was a risky move on her part. Because if he was

capable of causing harm, then she was placing herself as a target. She hoped the card interpretations she gave him sounded genuine, and not telling. What she didn't want was for him to think that she knew something and act upon it before she could set everything up.

Nana gathered the cards slowly as she felt the anger that was emanating from Bill. She could tell he was at the breaking point. When she tried to read his mind, she was so frightened that she shut it down immediately. He was thinking such horrible things she couldn't ... it was too much for her. He didn't respond for a while. Finally, he stood, and thanked Nana for the reading. He then excused himself, saying he was going to bed. Nana knew better.

Perfecto, now she could set her plan in motion.

Once he was gone, she texted Sheriff Fisher. It had been a while since they'd spoken, and she hoped he'd respond. Sure enough, he quickly replied to her text. She told him more or less what had happened, and let him know she felt that tonight Bill would try to do something to her. She suggested he send a plainclothesman to patrol the woods. When she was ready to walk Moro, she'd send him a text so the officer would be on guard.

Of course, just as she suspected, Sheriff Fisher told her that was too risky. He urged her not to go with the plan. If she knew for a fact, he was dangerous then they would come up with another plan. She apologized to Sheriff Fisher for jumping the gun, but she told him at this point she was certain Bill would act on his emotions. That meant tonight he would strike.

Not having much of a choice, Sheriff Fisher agreed to send a patrolman. However, he let her know he'd be in the Main House monitoring everything. Not many people knew, but Valdez had installed cameras along the trail. They were placed high above that no one knew they were there, but he could see anyone that was there allowing him to keep an eye out on Bill's movements.

After everything was organized, Nana told Moro they were going for a walk. She spotted the officer in the far distance just where Sheriff Fisher announced he'd be. Then she spoke to Moro along the path as if nothing was going on. Soon, she saw the shadow ... before she could act, he attacked.

Bill was so quick it took her by surprise even though she was expecting him. He quickly forced her on the ground, but was not able to do anything to her because Moro attacked him. He struggled to keep Moro at bay, but it was fruitless. Before he could proceed to actually hurt Nana, the police officer was there restraining him. Sheriff Fisher arrived within seconds.

"Stand up! You are under arrest for assault," the officer said as he called in for reinforcement.

Bill was crazed as he looked at Nana with daggers in his eyes. She knew it was finally over. He would never be able to hurt anyone again.

The police were able to confirm that once he set his eyes on someone the charm went on overdrive. Just as his victims became comfortable with him, he would come back and strangle them. Sheriff Fisher was even able to find evidence on two additional victims that had fallen prey to Bill Yardley.

After his arrest, with a search warrant in hand, they entered Bill's RV. There they found a bracelet Sasha had been wearing when she disappeared. That was not all they found. Hidden in the closet they found a souvenir box containing pictures of all of his victims. The police were finally able to tie him to several unsolved cases.

By the time he was brought before a judge, they had gathered enough evidence to prove that Bill was a serial killer and indeed the one that had killed Sasha. The evidence was overwhelming.

A few weeks later Nana heard from Beth; she was enjoying her visit with family. Sally on the other hand, had been convicted of murdering her husband. She lost all her money and the RV was donated to the campground. Mario left the campground one day, and never returned. Sally' conviction meant, she did what she did for nothing, because in the end she'd be sitting in a cell for a very long time.

All was finally good with the world. As November rolled around, the Miami Coastal Caravan Club had organized amongst those that stayed behind and the new members that had just arrived at the campground, a day trip to northern Vermont

Off they went on their excursion. By the end of the day everyone was exhausted, but everyone needed to eat. So, they picked a local restaurant that looked like the food was top notch. As they walked in the hostess greeted them and then it happened. They heard screams towards the back of the restaurant. Nana ran towards the noise as Moro barked.

When she found the source of the screams she abruptly stopped, and placed her hands over her mouth. There on the floor appeared to be a patron with a knife sticking out of her back.

Odd, she thought to herself, that woman is wearing the same outfit I'm wearing...

The End

Author's Note

LIST OF OTHER PUBLISHED AND UPCOMING
WORKS

❖

NOVELS:
Rosa The Cuban Psychic Paranormal Cozy Mysteries

- Book 1: A Fashionable Fate
- Book 2: A Parisian Bait
- Raul's Demise (Prequel)
- Book 3: A Mysterious Date

❖

A Tarot and Vintage Caravan Mystery Series

- Book 1: Murder at The Campground: A Cuban
  Cozy Mystery
- Book 2: Mystics, Murder and Mayhem in Crystal
  Falls : A Cuban Cozy Mystery
- Book 1.5: Corruption in Willowbrook Hollow: A
  Cuban Cozy Mystery Short Read

Wisterious Bay Cozy Paranormal Mystery Series

- Book 1: The Wisterious Witch
- Book 2: The Banished Reaper
- Book 3: A Humorous Skeleton

CHILDREN'S BOOKS:
Gizmo Adventures

- Gizmo Welcomes A New Baby

SHORT STORIES:
Holiday Corner Christmas Cozy Mystery

- Book 2: Ghostly Gift
- Book 4: Yuletide Murder

Small Town Big Magic Short Reads

- Book 1: Deadly Bakery
- Book 3: Library Conundrum

Upcoming
Lolita Restoration Mystery Series

- Book 1: If Walls Could Talk

❖

A Candeedo Brewdinkle Mystery Series

- Book 1: Cipher, Mobsters & A Sphynx

❖

Aunt Greneerie Mystery Series

- Book 1: Witching Hours and Mystical Whispers:
  The Adventures of Aunt Greneerie

❖

The Shoemaker Mystery Series

- Book 1: The Hidden Secret

❖

Notebooks

NOTEBOOKS:

- My Reading List
- My Tarot Journal
- My Notes - Las Cubanitas Journal
- My Notes - Cat Journal
- My Notes - Raul Journal
- My Notes - Candeedo Brewdinkle Journal
- My Notes - Abuela Nana from A Tarot and Vintage Caravan Journal
- My Notes - Dog Journal
- My Notes - Quirky Characters
- My Notes - Gizmo and Family Journal
- My Notes - Golf Journal
- My Notes - Rosa de Los Reyes Journal
- My Anxiety Journal
- My Aura Journal
- My Bird Watching Journal
- My Daily Journal
- My Notes Recipe Journal
- My Notes - Favorite Restaurants

Where to find me

Follow me on my various social media outlets including signing up for my Newsletter, and my Birthday Club.

❖

imrenfroe
Newsletter
Instagram
Twitter
Renfroe's Reading Room
Facebook Author Page
Facebook - Cozy Mystery Village

Author's Note

For the longest time, Ileana Muñoz-Renfroe wanted to be an author. Almost twenty years later, and after raising two children and owning numerous businesses, she decided to take the plunge.

Ileana was born in Cuba and raised in New York City's Washington Heights neighborhood. Yes, in The Heights, just as Lin-Manuel Miranda portrayed it—complete with abuelas spying over the neighborhood from their windowsill, Bodega owners welcoming you by name and chasing off graffiti artists, and everyone being involved in everyone's business. A large family who would gather every evening downstairs to watch the children play while the adults gossiped. It was welcoming and cozy.

In 2020, as Ileana sat in a Café in Paris, the idea of Rosa popped into her head, and the stories and characters became real. Since two of her passions are the paranormal and high-end fashion, she found a way to combine them and created Rosa The Cuban Psychic Mysteries. This series brings together her Cuban and American culture to make for a fun cozy mystery story. This is her debut novel.

She has also written a Children's Book – Gizmo

Welcomes a New Baby. Currently, she's hard at work illustrating several new books in the series. Ileana is excited about her designs and storyline.

When she is not writing, she enjoys traveling, reading, entertaining, and listening to music.

If you enjoyed reading Murder at The Campground: Book 1 - A Tarot and Vintage Caravan Cozy Mystery, please consider leaving a review.

Murder-Campground